# SOPHIE PEMBROKE

I've been dreaming, reading and writing romance for years, ever since I stayed up all night devouring Harlequin Mills and Boon novels as part of my English degree, and promptly gave up any pretext of enjoying tragic stories. After all, what's the point of a book without a happy ending? Born overseas, I grew up in Wales and now make my home in Hertfordshire with my scientist husband and our four year old, Alice in Wonderland obsessed, daughter. I keep a blog on my website, which should be about romance and writing, but is usually about cake and castles instead.

Follow me on Twitter at @Sophie_Pembroke.

ps*The Kiss Before Midnight*

SOPHIE PEMBROKE

Harper*Impulse* an imprint of
HarperCollins*Publishers* Ltd
77–85 Fulham Palace Road
Hammersmith, London W6 8JB

www.harpercollins.co.uk

A Paperback Original 2015

First published in Great Britain in ebook format by Harper*Impulse* 2014



Cover images © Shutterstock.com

Sophie Pembroke asserts the moral right
to be identified as the author of this work

A catalogue record for this book is
available from the British Library

ISBN: 978-0-00-812316-1

This novel is entirely a work of fiction.
The names, characters and incidents portrayed in it are
the work of the author's imagination. Any resemblance to
actual persons, living or dead, events or localities is
entirely coincidental.

Automatically produced by Atomik ePublisher from Easypress

# Chapter 1

**CHRISTMAS EVE EVE**

Molly Mackenzie couldn't help but think that free Prosecco in the office, while awesome in theory, might just end badly. She'd only been at the company for six months, and the bosses had already found reasons to celebrate at least once a fortnight on average. But usually they went down to the local pub, where the only electronics that stood to get damaged by spillages was the karaoke machine.

Molly knew she was still getting used to the idea of nine to five office work, but she hadn't honestly expected it to involve *more* alcohol than working in a hotel with two fully stocked bars.

"It's Christmas Eve Eve!" Jenna announced, sloshing bubbles over the side of her plastic cup as she hopped up to sit on Molly's desk. She leant back against the cubicle wall, and it groaned ominously.

"I'm not sure that Christmas Eve Eve is really a thing." Molly grabbed hold of the flimsy partition to try and keep it upright.

"Of course it is!" Jenna straightened up with indignation, and the cubicle wall creaked back into its usual position. "It's the eve of Christmas Eve, and well worthy of celebration. Hence the Prosecco."

Who could argue with that kind of logic? Grinning, Molly

lifted her own plastic glass to tap against Jenna's, sending another waterfall of bubbly over the edges of the overfilled cups. It might be miles away from her dad's traditional mulled wine, but it *was* tasty. Molly licked her fingers. No point wasting good Prosecco.

"Ooh, I think you're giving Bobby from accounts ideas," Jenna said, eyes wide.

Molly lowered her hand from her mouth. Quickly. "No time for ideas," she said, checking her watch.

"Are you sure?" Jenna asked, doubtfully. "He's pretty cute, you know."

Molly glanced over as casually as she could in the direction of the accounts team. They'd set up some sort of Prosecco fountain with a tower of plastic cups. Not exactly the Great Gatsby champagne saucer tower, especially since the glasses seemed to be held together with zebra print paperclips. Any interest the pretty cute Bobby had displayed had disappeared in the face of experiments with alcohol, and the chances were Jenna had been making it up anyway. Another thing Molly had learned over the last few months; if there was an office drama to be drummed up, Jenna would usually be behind it.

"I'm sure," Molly said. "Besides, even if I was interested, my train leaves in an hour. I need to head out soon." Especially given the light snow that had started falling half an hour ago. Her mum had been texting her weather updates all day. The last thing she needed, two days before Christmas, was to get stuck in the snow on a train somewhere. Almost home, but not quite.

She would miss her dad's mulled wine and mum's mince pies, for one thing.

Last Christmas, she'd been living at home, but a training course in Manchester had meant she only got home on Christmas Eve – the same day her brother Tim had arrived from Edinburgh. Their sister Dory had flown in from New York with her surprise new boyfriend on Christmas Day.

This year, Mum seemed very keen to have them all home and

safe before the twenty-fourth, to avoid any last minute surprises. Especially since it was the first time in seven years that Molly wouldn't be working either Christmas Day or New Year's Eve at the Liverpool hotel that had taken her on part-time at sixteen.

Tim was easy; he'd moved back in with their parents when his contract ended in Edinburgh that summer – conveniently two short weeks after Molly moved to London. And Dory and Lucas's flight should be landing any time now.

It was going to be the perfect family Christmas.

Jenna groaned. "God, how long are you going to be gone again?"

"Until the second of January." Just like Molly had told her eighty-four times already.

Jenna's despair grew more dramatic, her drink tilting dangerously close to Molly's computer. "That's forever! You're going to miss everything fun about living in London over the holidays. My New Year's Eve party most of all! It's the *only* place to be in London on December 31st."

Molly wasn't entirely convinced Jenna's party actually rivalled Trafalgar Square or fireworks on the South Bank, but she let her friend keep her illusions. "Sorry." She gave her an apologetic smile because it was easier than explaining that, actually, there was no place she'd rather be this Christmas than home with her family. Well, her family and Jake.

"You know I'd love to be there," she went on, "but I've got family stuff to do. My sister and her boyfriend will be over from the States, so my parents are planning another big party for New Year's Eve, since last year's was such a success."

Well, for most people anyway. For Molly it had managed to be simultaneously one of the best – and then worst – parties ever. All thanks to Jake Sommers.

Jenna leant in closer, her eyebrows knitting with suspicion. "Your family. That's the whole and only reason you're going home for ten long days."

"Nine and a bit, really." Just enough time to soak up all the family-ness, that feeling of home, before she came back to London.

"You're avoiding the question." Jenna straightened up, her eyes wide, and waved her Prosecco at Molly accusingly. "It's not your family at all, is it? You've got a guy waiting at home for you! It all makes sense now."

"Jenna, you know I'm single. Unless you count Bing Crosby singing White Christmas on the stereo, the only guys waiting at home for me are my dad and my brother." Although, she couldn't deny the rather expensive, definitely lacy and barely there lingerie she'd stuffed into the top of her case that morning, in a last minute fit of optimism.

Jenna kept staring, and Molly felt the lie start to strain and then break inside her. "Well, and Jake, I suppose. But he's practically family." Except for how last Christmas, Molly had suddenly looked at Jake in a totally different way to how she looked at Tim, her *actual* brother.

"A secret family member you've never ever mentioned before, even though I've heard everything about your brother and sister and your great-aunt Mabel!" Was it the Prosecco or the indignation making Jenna's voice rise in volume with every word?

"People are staring," Molly muttered, trying not to catch the eye of any members of their audience. How weird was it that Jenna could be her closest friend in London, and not know about Jake? Lara, her actual best friend, had known him almost as long as Molly had. And had been the first person she'd called on New Year's Day to tell her everything.

"Then you better start telling me all about Jake, hadn't you? Before I start *asking more questions.*" Jenna shouted the last part for extra effect.

Molly downed her Prosecco. "Okay. Fine. Jake is Tim's best friend – has been since they were, like, five – before I was even born. His parents died when he and Tim were eighteen, just before they left for uni, so Mum and Dad invited him to ours for Christmas that year. He doesn't have any other family, really, so we've just sort of adopted him into ours, ever since." She shrugged. "He's part of home for me. No big deal."

Jenna's eyes narrowed. "That's it. He's like a brother to you. And there's never been even a hint of anything more between you?"

How did Jenna always manage to zero in on the things Molly didn't want to admit to? Like the slight lie on her CV about her fluency in French, or the fact that she accidentally kissed Stefan from marketing after one too many tequila shots at the karaoke bar six weeks ago?

"I knew it!" Jenna declared triumphantly. "You're blushing. Tell all, immediately."

Dammit! Fair skin and a huge capacity for embarrassment just wasn't a fair combination.

"Fine." Molly dumped her empty glass on a passing tray, carried by one of the senior account managers, and snagged another full one. "So we might have kissed. Just a little bit. Last New Year's Eve."

Understatement of the year.

"And this New Year's Eve…?" Jenna leered at her, just a little bit.

Molly shrugged. "Probably nothing. I haven't seen him since, and we've never talked about it. We were both pretty drunk. He might not even remember."

Even if Molly was never going to forget. How could she? The slide of his hands up her arms, then down to her waist. The heat of his mouth on hers. The strength of his chest, pressing up against her. The wall at her back the only thing holding her up.

No. If Jake had forgotten all of that he wasn't human. Or – and the thought sent a cold shiver running through her – it hadn't been as incredible for him.

"I think you're giving up too easily," Jenna said, leaning back on her hands, her Prosecco finished and thoughts of another drink long since abandoned for the obviously more interesting pastime of tormenting Molly. "I think you should go after him."

Molly shook her head, trying to forget about the ridiculous lingerie in her bag. "It's a bad idea." Even if her subconscious obviously thought it was a good one. And, she had to admit, it hadn't *seemed* bad, in the early hours of January first, with tequila still coursing through her veins and the heady lust of possibility making it impossible to think straight.

"Why?" Jenna's eyes widened. "Was it that bad?"

"No," Molly groaned. "It was that good."

"Then what's the problem?"

The problem, of course, was what had happened next. The door had opened and Jake had wrenched himself away before anyone saw them. By the time Molly had managed to open her eyes properly, he was gone, and her brother was staring at her with suspicion.

Jake had avoided her the rest of the night.

"He's not interested," Molly said, wishing her friend wouldn't push the point – but knowing she probably would.

"He kissed you. That's a pretty good indicator of interest."

"Apparently not." She'd believed it could be, for the first couple of days, and had even made a stupid resolution – to get Jake into bed by the end of the year. But then he'd failed to reply to her most casual, long time friend texts, and hadn't even shown up to her 'Molly's Moving to London!' party.

She might not always be that great at subtle, but even Molly could take a hint that heavy.

Jenna frowned, and reached out to steal Molly's cup for a sip of Prosecco. "This is actually a thing, isn't it? I mean, I was just teasing, but you actually have a thing for this guy, don't you?"

"No. Absolutely not." Molly grabbed her drink back.

"Liar. I bet you've been lusting after him since puberty."

Except she really, really hadn't. It was just this last year that she seemed to have gone crazy – the first year in forever when she hadn't seen Jake with any kind of regularity. Maybe this was just absence making the heart grow… lustful.

"No." Molly spoke firmly, then winced. "Just the last twelve months."

"Aha!" Jenna pointed a slightly wobbly finger at her, and Molly buried her head in her arms on the desk. One kiss, and she'd lost her mind over a man who'd only ever been a friend.

"I know, I know, I'm pathetic." The words came out rather muffled, thanks to the fluffy cardigan she'd thrown over her work dress that day.

"Not pathetic." Jenna tugged on her hair to make her look up. "You just need a plan to get what you want."

"You think?" Was that hope in her voice? God, she really *was* pathetic. How clear did the guy need to make it that he wasn't interested before she moved on?

And no, kissing Stefan at karaoke *really* didn't count as moving on. Not least because it hadn't caused even one per cent of the tingles her hurried encounter with Jake had.

"So, he's going to be there all Christmas, right?" Jenna asked.

Molly nodded. "Normally he just arrives on Christmas Eve and leaves on Boxing Day – he doesn't live that far away, and his office is in the city. But with Tim moving away to Switzerland for his new job in January, I think mum said she'd talked Jake into staying with us until New Year's Day."

"Perfect! That gives you nine and a bit days to win him over." Jenna smiled in a way that Molly had already come to mistrust. "In fact, I'm going to set you a holiday challenge. Your mission, and you have no choice but to accept it, is to seduce that man! And then come back and tell me all about it, obvs."

"What, are you going to double dog dare me?" Molly asked, forcing a laugh. She wasn't serious, right?

"If I have to!" Jenna leant closer, as if about to impart some vital, probably inebriated, wisdom. "Look. You've been a single girl in London for more than six months now, yeah? And you've barely shown a hint of interest in anyone - apart from that blip with Stefan at the karaoke. Which means that being hung up on this Jake guy is affecting your chances of meeting a great guy and having some incredible sex. Right?"

Molly blinked. "You think that if I sleep with Jake over Christmas it will enable me to have more sex with other men down here in London next year?"

"Exactly!" Jenna patted her on the head like a proud teacher.

"There's a flaw in this plan somewhere." Except, she was a grown up now, right? Twenty-three, single, living it up in London. She had a proper job in a real office – not just working the same reception desk at the same hotel she'd been a chambermaid at when she was sixteen. She could totally do one-night stands and meaningless flings, right? Especially since she no longer lived with her parents.

So why hadn't she? Could it be because of one stupid kiss with Jake? Maybe she did need to get him out of her system.

"Don't be pessimistic!" Stealing Molly's cup of Prosecco, Jenna hopped off the desk. "Come on, you're going to miss your train. Go forth and seduce that man!"

Laughing, Molly stood, pushed her chair under her desk, double checked her out of office autoreply was on and shut down her computer.

"And I want a full debrief the moment you get back," Jenna added, pulling up the handle of Molly's case and handing it to her. "So don't get too attached – you've got a life here now, remember?"

"If there's anything to report, I promise you'll hear it." It was a fairly safe promise, Molly decided. After all, the chances of her managing to get Jake alone long enough in her parents' four-bed terrace in the suburbs, with Dory and Lucas *and* Tim all home too, were phenomenally slim.

"Merry Christmas everyone!" Molly called out, as she headed for the front door. "See you in the New Year."

When, no doubt, everything would be exactly the same as it was now. Unless she did something to change that.

# Chapter 2

Molly couldn't forget Jenna's dare as she lugged her suitcase down the escalator towards the Northern Line, shaking the snow from her hair as she went. Even amongst the crowd of Christmas Eve Eve travellers, with the scarf that had been essential outside in the winter chill now making her overheated neck itch, she couldn't help but remember that kiss, one more time.

Come to think of it, the memory probably wasn't helping the overheating any more than the overcrowded tube was. She had to put Jake Sommers completely out of her head, and focus on her journey home.

She stood all the way to Euston, crammed up against the door and clutching the handle of her suitcase for dear life, then struggled up the escalator into the overground station. Dragging her case behind her, she wove through the holiday season crush, past at least ten people in Santa hats and avoiding a group of guys in suits warbling Silent Night, all the way to platform five.

The queue to get onto the train stretched right back to the main concourse, and Molly mentally thanked her mother for insisting she book ahead to make sure she got a seat. Sure, she thought as she handed her ticket to the inspector, there would probably be someone sitting in it by the time she got there, but hopefully the festive spirit would prevail and they'd give it up once she waved her ticket in their face.

The only problem was, once she was settled into her window seat, with the businessman beside her tapping away on his laptop, there wasn't much *to* do but watch the snowflakes drifting down outside and think about Jake.

Not just Jake, though. That line in her diary, the one she always started keeping daily on the first of January and slipped to monthly updates around mid February. The last line under the heading *Goals For The Year.*

The first two goals she'd actually knocked off by the summer. New job? Check. Move to London? Check.

But goal number three, which should have been the easiest of them all if that December 31st kiss had been anything to go by, had remained elusive.

Sleep with Jake Sommers.

A little hard to achieve when she hadn't actually been in the same room as him all year, and not even in the same city most of the time.

Why had she even added that to the list anyway? Without it, she was two for two on the real, important things she wanted to achieve that year. Getting away from Liverpool and starting her own, grown up life in London had been a goal for so long that she'd started to doubt she'd ever make it. But she had. On her own terms, without any help from anyone.

Sure, maybe her tiny shared flat wasn't a New York penthouse with weekends on a charmingly rustic farm with a fabulously gorgeous rich American, like Dory had somehow landed, but it was hers and she'd made it there herself. And that counted for a hell of a lot, especially to Molly.

But still, the last goal at the front of her journal nagged at her. She couldn't pretend she hadn't set it; that wasn't how things worked. Every New Year's Eve when they were kids, Molly, Dory and Tim had huddled together in the girls' room to make their resolutions. Sometimes they were joke ones – like the year Tim resolved to convince their mum to believe in aliens. Sometimes they were things that mattered, like exams and friendships. And sometimes they'd forced them on each other, like the year she and Dory ganged up to make Tim give up smoking when he was fifteen.

They'd stopped some years ago, and Molly wasn't even really sure why. Probably it had something to do with them all being in different places for New Year – different friends, different jobs, different parties, even different cities. But Molly always set her goals for the year – even though her track record for meeting them wasn't great. This year was the first year she stood a chance at a clean sweep. But not with the memory of Jake Sommers's kiss and the unfulfilled resolution hanging over her head.

Outside the window, the snow that had been light and magical in London was growing heavier and more threatening. Beside her, Mr Businessman stopped clicking keys long enough to look up and say, "Well, it looks like getting a taxi will be fun tonight."

Molly wasn't worried about taxis. Her dad drove one of those, for heaven's sake. But if he was out on a job and the *trains* stopped running then she might be in trouble. Well, not trouble, exactly. Dad would drive into the city to pick her up from Lime Street station if the local line shut down, but it wouldn't be fun for either of them. Liverpool city centre two days before Christmas was *not* a place anyone wanted to drive around if they didn't have to. Especially since she knew her dad had taken Christmas week off to spend with the family.

"I'm practically retired now, Moll," he'd said, last time she called. "What's the point of getting to my age if you can't sit back and enjoy it, eh?"

Which didn't mean he wouldn't do a few jobs, when it suited him, Molly knew. Especially on the days when it was to his benefit to be out from under her mother's feet.

*"Ladies and gentlemen, I am sorry to report that due to the inclement weather, there will be no local or national trains departing from our final stop, Liverpool Lime Street. There will be staff on hand*

*to advise you on local hotels and taxi firms, and we hope to have all services running again tomorrow morning."* The crackly announcement sent waves of muttering through the carriage.

"Damn it," Molly murmured, reaching for her phone. She'd *known* she should have booked an earlier train, but Jenna had been adamant that she couldn't miss the work drinks that evening.

She tried the home phone first, but there was no reply. Firing off a text to her mum, she called Tim next.

"What's up sis?" The sound of a fruit machine paying out in the background put pay to any hopes of her brother picking her up.

"You're in the pub?" Maybe he'd be somewhere in the city centre and they could travel home together. That could work. He could carry her damn suitcase for one thing. Brothers had to have some uses, right?

"Yeah." He said it as if anyone with half a brain would be. "It's Christmas Eve Eve. Why aren't you?"

"You know Christmas Eve Eve isn't really a thing, right? Never mind. Look, I'm on the train into Lime Street now, but the trains to Crosby aren't running. Which pub are you in?"

"The George and Dragon. Wanted to be within staggering distance. Hey! Guess who's here tonight!"

"Someone sober enough to pick me up from Lime Street?" Molly asked, without much hope.

"God, no. You're shit out of luck there, sorry. No, Lara's here! Wanna talk to her?" He passed the phone over before he could reply.

"Tell me you're nearly home!" Lara yelled down the phone. "I need my best friend back!"

"Almost," Molly promised. "Or I would be if I could get someone to pick me up from Lime Street. Are you going to come round tomorrow?"

"Have I ever missed mulled wine and mince pies at your parents' house on Christmas Eve?" Lara asked, making it clear through her tone that Molly was an idiot for asking.

"Not willingly," Molly admitted. "Good. I can tell you all about

London.”

"Yeah. Great. Here's Tim." The phone line went muffled, then crackly, then Tim was back.

"Is she okay?" Molly asked, frowning at her reflection in the window. "She sounded… off."

"That'll be the cinnamon flavoured vodka," Tim guessed. "They've got this special offer on tonight. I have to tell you about it—"

"Tim," Molly interrupted. "I kind of had a reason for calling. The about to be stuck in Lime Street thing? Do you know where Dad is? No one's answering at home."

"He's gone to pick up Dory and whatshisname from Manchester airport. Guess he might be a while if the weather's bad."

"Lucas. You know his name is Lucas." A while, in this case, could mean anything up to a couple of days. Damn it.

"Yeah, whatever. And Mum's over at Auntie Susan's at some sort of girls' party thing. Ann Summers or what have you."

"It's a cooking party," Molly said, finally remembering. "And God, thanks for that image." She sighed. "Okay, well, if you speak to either of them, tell them I'll try and get a taxi home, if I can find one in this weather." She dreaded to think how much it would cost, but she just wanted to get home. It was Christmas, after all.

"No, hang on Moll." Tim sounded suddenly sober, the big brother swooping in to take care of things again. She should be grateful, Molly knew. After all, hadn't she called hoping for his help? But the assumption that she couldn't even be trusted to get a taxi on her own grated.

"It's fine, Tim. You've been drinking, and so has Mum probably." It was Christmas, after all. Half of Britain was probably plastered. "Dad's miles away. I can just grab a taxi. It'll be fine."

"Just wait a min. I'll call you back in five." The phone went dead in her hand. Apparently it was Super Tim to the rescue again.

Fingers still wrapped around her phone, she stared back out of the window. The flakes were bigger, heavier now, like the granddaddies of the little flurries they'd had in London. These snowflakes meant business.

"Well, at least it will be a white Christmas," she whispered to herself. Dad would be pleased. He always complained that it wasn't really Christmas without a snowman in the back garden.

She jumped as her phone buzzed, but it was a text, not a call.

*Couldn't get through – are you in a tunnel? Anyway, all sorted. He'll be there to pick you up at Lime Street when you arrive. See you in the pub! Tx*

He? Which he?

Molly felt her breath start to freeze in her lungs as she realised there was only one person Tim would call for a favour like this on Christmas Eve Eve.

Jake Sommers.

# Chapter 3

Jake ended the phone call with rather more than the required force, cursing hands free technology for the first time in its existence. He'd almost ignored the call from Tim anyway – not because he didn't want to talk to his best friend, but because he knew Tim was in the pub, probably sloshed, and Jake was going to *be* there in an hour or so, anyway. What did they need to talk about at this point? They had a whole week of festivities to enjoy together. Himself, Tim and Tim's family, all pretending that Jake was one of them, even when everyone knew he wasn't.

He was, as ever, the poor orphan child, given a place out of the snow with mulled wine and mince pies and happy people, for the holidays.

Not that he was complaining – far from it. Without the Mackenzies, he'd have no family at all. He was happy to take what he could get – and grateful that what he'd been able to get was as warm, welcoming and loving as Tim's family.

But it did come with a sense of obligation – one he suspected was probably entirely in his head. Still, it meant that when Tim called, he answered. And when Tim asked him to pick up his little sister from Lime Street station on a snowy Christmas Eve Eve (as if that were even a real thing) he said yes, no questions asked. Because Molly should be like a little sister to him, too, given everything the family had done for him over the years.

Jake cursed the still falling snow. Because thinking of Molly as a little sister? Practically impossible these days.

He tried. Really he did. In the twelve months since he'd last seen her, he'd listened to Tim and his parents talking about how well she was doing, how her move to London could be the making of her, and all he could think was that she was two hundred miles further away from him now.

He had yet to decide if that were a good thing or not, but he knew his body had very strong feelings on the matter.

His body's feelings were why he'd been avoiding her. Why he hadn't even been able to go to her leaving party, making excuses about being away with work instead. Why, whenever he'd been working down in London this year, he'd ignored the scrawled address Tim had given him, tucked in the back of his work folder.

He'd always known that he had an issue with temptation. All the things he knew were a bad idea – one more drink, staying out just a bit later, chasing that girl he knew would break his heart… Jake just wasn't very good at saying no. As a teenager, he'd spent a lot of time giving in to temptation – especially after his parents died. But, after five years of hard study at university, he hadn't wanted to jeopardise that during his two years of on the job experience before he qualified as an architect.

So slowly, he'd started resisting. Going home when he'd promised himself he would. Knowing his limits. Turning down the opportunities that looked fun, but he knew would bring more trouble than anything else, in the end.

Which was just as well, really, as it was that year, when he came home for Christmas, that he'd suddenly realised that Molly wasn't a little girl, or an awkward teen anymore. Away at university herself then, she'd grown into the sort of woman he'd buy a drink in a bar, charm, and take home for the night.

The thought of other men doing that to sweet little Molly Mackenzie made something burn, deep inside him.

But it wasn't something he could do anything about. She was a grown woman, and not quite his sister, but close enough. Close enough, that he could never dream of being that guy in the bar, but not so close that he could pull the big brother card and keep her safe from those sleazebags.

So, he'd become an expert at resisting temptation, knowing that if he gave in once, he'd give in forever – on everything. He'd held himself in check, over and over – until last New Year's Eve.

Jake's lips tightened as he swerved the car into the station car park, flakes still falling fast and thick on his windscreen. Twelve months of trying to forget the moment he'd let down his guard and given in to that temptation, and here he was, forced by his own rules of family and obligation to spend time alone in an enclosed space with the woman.

The woman whose mouth he could still taste under his, if he didn't concentrate on forgetting. Whose curves he could still feel pressed up against him. Whose soft, sweet skin still kept him awake at night.

It was, Jake had found, much harder to forget those things when he was alone in the dark.

It was dark now, night having swooped down with the snow at four thirty. The glitter of snowflakes in the streetlights gave Liverpool's station a magical glow it couldn't claim to possess most of the year. He parked his car where he was pretty sure there were some double yellow lines hidden by the snow, and was about to call Molly's mobile – a number he'd had programmed in his phone since the day she got it, but had never actually used – when he saw a figure hopping down the steps outside the station. Despite the knitted hat pulled down over her wavy auburn hair, and the thick grey coat hiding her body, he knew her instantly.

She was almost at the car before he realised he should get out and help her. God, he was failing at more than just resisting temptation today.

"Hey," he said, stepping out of the car. Cold, wet misery seeped into his socks over the top of his probably now ruined leather shoes. He held back a wince. "Need a hand with that?"

Molly flashed him a smile that shone brighter than the snow under the streetlights. "I've got it."

She popped open the boot and heaved her oversized suitcase inside without much effort, while Jake hung back with wet feet and a general feeling of uselessness. He had to get a handle on whatever it was that made him so… un-Jake-like in her presence. Yeah, so he'd kissed her. But she was still just Molly. Just Tim's kid sister. The girl who'd hung around and bugged them when they were teenagers.

The woman he'd pressed up against the wall of her childhood bedroom, his mouth firm and wanting against hers…

No. He really, really couldn't be thinking about that right now.

Slipping around to the other side of the car, he opened the passenger door for her, unable to keep his gaze from fixing on the line of her neck under her hair, and the single snowflake that had landed on her skin and was melting, trailing down her throat, under the collar of her coat…

Swallowing, Jake forced a smile as Molly slid into her seat, slamming the door behind her rather harder than he'd intended.

Back in the driver's seat, he checked his mirrors obsessively, and prepared to pull out, very aware of all the extra hazards the weather presented.

"Thanks for coming to get me," Molly said, and he risked a glance up at her. Her lip was caught between her teeth, plump and pink, and it made him want to kiss it, so damn much. "You really didn't have to. Although I don't suppose Tim gave you much of a choice."

"You know your brother," Jake replied, before he realised that sounded like he hadn't want to come and fetch her. Which, actually, he hadn't. But he didn't want her to know that. "And it's fine. I was nearby, anyway." Sort of. Well, not really.

"No you weren't." Molly smiled, and Jake stopped paying full attention to the road for a second, before wrenching his gaze back through the windscreen. A second was all it took to cause an accident – hadn't he learnt that lesson from his parent's death? He couldn't allow himself to be distracted by a pretty smile, or anything else, while driving. Okay, fine, a stunning, heart stopping smile.

"How do you know that?" he asked, not looking at her.

"I can tell." She shuffled around in her seat a bit, obviously getting comfortable, her huge leather bag settled on her knee. Between that and her case, she must have been loaded down, getting to the station alone.

Suddenly, Jake felt a spike of guilt in his chest. Why hadn't he offered to come and pick Molly up anyway? Just because he was undergoing a particularly strong surge of unbrotherly-like feelings, didn't mean she should have to suffer. It just meant he needed to control them better.

"How can you tell?" he asked, because that didn't make any sense at all.

Molly shrugged. "I've known you too long, Jake. I can tell when you're lying."

Jake's shoulders froze, his hands gripping the steering wheel too tightly. If that was true, he was definitely in trouble.

Suddenly, he really, really wanted to get to the pub with Tim. And take a long, cold walk home afterwards.

–

Okay, this was weird. Molly's gaze fixed on Jake's white knuckles, clenching the steering wheel for dear life. Did he always drive like this? She didn't remember him doing so, but then, his parents *had* died in a car crash. Maybe that made him nervous. Or it could just be the snow – it had to be pretty treacherous to drive in. Not that she'd ever tried.

Or maybe, just maybe, it was her doing that.

Running her gaze up his arms, she took in the jumper he was wearing – a red one she thought her mum had bought him last year – and the hard lines of his shoulders under it. Almost as if he were steeling himself for something.

Probably, a conversation with her about what happened last New Year's Eve.

In fact, he was probably rehearsing it in his head. Getting his 'I love you like a sister, I'm sorry if I ever gave you the impression of something more' lines straight, all ready for her.

Well. That just didn't suit Molly's purposes at all.

"Are you all ready for Christmas?" she asked, a determinedly cheery note in her voice.

"Uh, yes. I think so." His head turned, just slightly, as he glanced at her, and Molly saw the surprise in his expression. "You?"

"Mostly." She sighed. "I have a lot of wrapping to do tomorrow, though. Just hoping that Mum's bought extra paper, as usual."

"I'm sure she will have," Jake said, although from the puzzlement in his voice Molly suspected that he'd had all his presents' gift wrapped when he ordered them online. That was his usual M.O.

She hunkered down in her seat a bit more. He was a successful architect now, in high demand across the country. He could probably afford that convenience, more than he could spare the time to actually go shopping himself. He certainly wouldn't have spent hours trawling the tiny independent stores of north London looking for the perfect, purse friendly, present for every family member.

A reminder of just how different they were. It was easy to forget, sometimes. To think that Jake was just another member of the family, brought up by a taxi driver and a teacher, just like Tim. But he wasn't. He came from a family of high earning professionals, and he'd continued the trend. He'd sold his parents' home and built himself a new one, pocketing the cash that came from selling a house in an up-and-coming suburb and heading out to the fancier county of Cheshire, a forty minute drive away.

Molly stared out the window at the snowflakes again, feeling their chill this time more than she had on the train. Shouldn't this feel more like home, now she was so close? And it wasn't like the expensive heating system of Jake's sleek car couldn't overcome the cold. But suddenly she felt like she wasn't quite a fit in either place – London or Liverpool. And certainly not here, in a too expensive car with a man who was embarrassed by how much he'd wanted her, once.

The Prosecco had worn off hours ago, and suddenly Jenna's plan seemed ridiculous.

*Of course* she wasn't going to be able to seduce Jake Sommers before midnight on New Year's Eve. And she'd humiliate herself beyond the telling of it if she even tried.

The only problem was that this didn't make her want to try any less.

They drove in silence for longer than was really comfortable, until the house and streets around them became familiar, and Molly knew they were nearly home. As they approached The George and Dragon, she realised that her window of opportunity to talk to Jake alone, without her entire family trying to eavesdrop, was closing rapidly.

"Pull over here," she blurted out, without really processing the thought first.

Jake raised an eyebrow, but turned carefully into the pub car park, which wasn't quite what Molly had intended but would do in a pinch.

"You want to go see Tim first?" Jake asked, cutting the engine.

"No. Well, yes, maybe, actually." No one would be home, she realised, unless mum had headed back early because of the snow. They could totally have had this conversation at the house, in private, without snow clogging up their windows and making things even more claustrophobic than ever.

"O-kay." Jake frowned, a puzzled line forming between his brows. "I'll be honest, Moll, I'm not following."

Moll. He'd called her that as a child, as a girl, as the annoying tagalong little sister of his best friend. When he'd kissed her, he'd called her Molly, drawing the word out like her pleasure.

Clearly, they were back to annoying sister territory.

"Look, I don't mind if we go see Tim or not. I just wanted… before we see everyone else and it's all family all the time and everyone is listening and stuff. Do we, I don't know, do we need to talk about last New Year's Eve?" The words burbled out of her until she wasn't sure they even formed a full sentence. But the way Jake's face stiffened up, his frown lines deeper than ever, she knew he understood what she meant.

She held her breath and waited for an answer.

# Chapter 4

Of course she wanted to talk. Jake had never met a woman who didn't. Who couldn't just move on and repress like a normal person.

"It was a year ago, Moll. Can't we just chalk it up to too much of Tim's tequila and forget about it?"

"Sure," she said, in the sort of voice that made it very clear that she wasn't sure at all. "If that's what you want."

"I'm not saying… all I mean is… it's not like that has to, you know. Change anything, I guess." God, he sounded like her. Was babbling catching? He'd never had to worry about it before.

"I didn't mean, well, change. I just… you've been avoiding me this year."

Jake winced. Kind of hard to deny that one. It was a miracle no one else had called him on it, really. "Not avoiding, not really," he lied. "I just didn't want things to be weird for you."

"It was weird not having you at my goodbye party." Molly sounded so small and sad; he felt the guilt that had needled him that whole night pricking him again.

"I'm sorry. I should have been there." A true brother would have been. One who wasn't harbouring inappropriate thoughts about his almost-sister.

"Yes, you should." She flashed him a quick, sharp smile. "So, if we're making things not weird… how do you suggest we go about that?"

"Well, not kissing again should help." Why had he said that? Oh God, really, had he lost control of his mouth altogether? Because as he said the words, his gaze dipped automatically to her lips. Her tongue darted out to moisten them, and he could almost taste her by just watching and remembering. And now kissing her was the only thing in the world he could think about doing.

"That should be easy enough I guess." Was her voice really so breathy, or was his imagination messing with him?

"Yeah. I mean we managed it for twenty-plus years before, right?"

"Exactly." Was she staring at his mouth, too? Why couldn't they have had this conversation in the house, preferably with her parents in the next room as a constant, painful reminder why he shouldn't be doing this? Or even thinking about it.

"So, we'll just go back to being… friends."

"Yeah. Friends." With the memory of how close he'd come to stripping off every inch of her clothing still fresh – not to mention how much he still wanted to do so – he really wasn't going anywhere near 'I'm like your brother.'

"Who just happened to, well—"

"Yeah. That." Jake cut her off. If he heard her say the words there was no way he'd be able to keep up with the resisting.

"Okay then," Molly said, and Jake nodded.

Which meant the conversation should be over. They'd decided everything they needed to, agreed to put things behind them. So why were they still in the car park? Why were her eyes still so dark in the light of the falling snow? Why were these car seats so damn close?

"Jake…"

She didn't need to say any more. He could read every iota of longing in her eyes. Could she see it in his? Saying the words was one thing, but sticking by them? A whole different proposition.

He was going to tell her *no*. Really he was.

Except a banging on the window interrupted him.

"Hey, you two! Excellent timing!" As the snow slipped down the windscreen, Tim's beaming face appeared; he was clearly plastered and full of Christmas spirit. "Saved me a walk home!"

"Guess we're not going to the pub, then," Jake muttered, as he opened the car door. Which was a shame, because he could really, really use a drink around now.

Molly watched Tim and Jake undertake a snowy man hug, before her brother stumbled into the back of the car, tipping almost entirely sideways as he grinned at her.

"Moll! You made it! At least I'll have one sister home for Christmas this year."

"Dory will be here too," Molly pointed out, only half paying attention. Jake had settled back into the driver's seat, and she could smell his aftershave. It make her want to lick down the line of his throat, and she really couldn't be having those thoughts in the presence of her brother, however drunk and oblivious he was.

"Not if her plane gets snowed in and can't land." Tim sprawled across the backseat as Jake started up the engine again. "Then it'll just be the three of us and Mum and Dad."

"More mince pies for me, then," Jake said, not even glancing over at Molly. She tried not to feel offended by that.

He'd been about to kiss her, she was sure of it. Or, in honesty, she'd have totally kissed him. One way or another, kissing had been about to happen.

And now it wasn't.

"She'll get here," Molly said, staring out at the snow. "You know Dory. She won't let a bit of weather get her down." After all, this was perfect Dory they were talking about. The over achieving big sister who had departed for London the moment she graduated from university and landed the sort of job mum could boast about. Then, not satisfied with that, she'd moved to New York for her dream job and dream fiancé. And then – then! The ultimate insult to less successful younger siblings – she'd lost it all, lied to her family for *months,* and still somehow managed to return home for Christmas last year with a rich, gorgeous, besotted boyfriend and the promise of an even better job lined up.

It really, really wasn't fair.

Tim had almost dozed off in the backseat by the time Jake pulled into the driveway of her parents' house. Her dad's cab was still missing, but the lights were on in the kitchen and lounge, which meant that mum had to be home. Philippa Mackenzie was obsessive about turning everything off before she left the house – even unplugging small appliances – in case of fire. The Christmas tree lights in the front window wouldn't be twinkling if she wasn't there.

"Are you ready?" she murmured to Jake as the car stopped. She wasn't even really sure what she meant by that – but he seemed to know. His face, so smooth and expressionless on the drive from the pub, suddenly tightened, and the nod he gave her was too sharp, too precise.

Was this hard for him too? Not really knowing where they stood? It seemed to be.

That made Molly feel ever so slightly better about the whole thing.

She got out of the car first, treading carefully on the snow to get to the boot and pull out her case. The last thing she needed was Jake being chivalrous and carrying it for her – the chances were that, the way she felt tonight, it would send her hormones into overdrive and she'd throw herself at him right there and then. Which would mean her brother and probably her mum would witness her humiliation when her advances were knocked back.

Except… for that one, brief moment in the car, before Tim interrupted, Jake had wanted to kiss her, she was almost sure of it. Which meant there was something making him hold back. It couldn't just be the little sister thing, could it?

Well, whatever it was, she had eight days to find out and convince him it didn't matter.

"Let me help you with that," Jake said, suddenly at her side.

Molly gripped her suitcase a little tighter. "I'm fine, really. Haven't you got your own bag?" She knew he had – she'd seen the expensive looking leather holdall in the boot when she put her case in.

"Yeah, but…" Jake reached out for the handle again, and she realised this wasn't for her benefit anyway. It was for her family's. To show that he was a perfect gentleman, as always. Couldn't have them suspecting he ever had other intentions now, could he?

Molly yanked the case away from him but the movement proved too much for her ancient suitcase. Zip splitting across the side, the overstuffed case bled its contents across the snowy drive – sexy lingerie first.

Behind her, Tim laughed, and Molly's face grew redder as she tried to stuff her belongings back inside. *Way to look desperate, Molly.*

"I don't think you'll be needing that at home for the holidays, Moll!" She gritted her teeth at her brother's amusement, very aware of Jake crouched beside her trying to help, his gaze and hands studiously avoiding anything slippery, silk or lacy.

But as she reached for the last few items, Jake glanced up and she couldn't help but catch his eye. Something burned deep in that gaze, and it wasn't embarrassment. He'd seen what she'd packed and jumped to the obvious – and correct – conclusion that it was for him.

So much for the element of surprise.

Jake Sommers knew exactly what she wanted from him this Christmas – and most intriguingly of all, he seemed slightly more wanting than resistant.

Suddenly her malfunctioning suitcase seemed more like an opportunity than an embarrassment.

# Chapter 5

As Jake tried to tear his gaze away from Molly's, the front door flew open and suddenly, the warmth of home reached out through the snow and found them, even in the freezing night. In an instant, Molly had forgotten all about him, Jake could tell. Yanking it closed, she dragged her suitcase along, leaving wheel marks in the snow, racing towards her mother and the smell of mince pies baking, and wine mulling on the stove. Jake couldn't blame her. *This* was Christmas. Everything else could wait – especially the interloper who didn't really belong anyway.

"You made it!" Philippa Mackenzie threw her arms around her daughter the moment she came within reach, and Molly dropped her case to the ground to return the hug. Stepping to the side, out of the way, Jake picked it up for her. "And my boy!" Philippa moved onto the slightly staggering Tim.

"Mum. You saw me earlier. I *live* here." Tim squirmed away slightly, and Jake felt an ache in his chest.

"I know. But only for nine more days. And besides, it's Christmas." The reasoning that would rule for those nine days, Jake knew. The Mackenzies took Christmas *very* seriously.

"And you!" Philippa pushed Tim aside to get to Jake, and he braced himself for impact. Beside him, Tim leant against the wall for extra support. "It's been months since we saw you! Far,

far too long." She gave Jake a hug that he knew would be every bit as warm and tight as the ones she'd given her blood children. But still, he couldn't relax. Couldn't sink into the hug like Molly and Tim had done.

Couldn't believe he really belonged in this place, with these people. Especially given what he'd just been imagining doing to their daughter.

*Don't think about Molly's underwear. Just… don't. Especially not while hugging her mother.*

That way, madness lay.

Finally, Philippa released him, and he exhaled at last. "Now, let's get you three inside. Your dad left me in charge of the mulled wine when he left for the airport, and I've just got a fresh batch of mince pies out of the oven."

Perfect. Mulled wine, mince pies and Bing Crosby on the stereo. The traditional Mackenzie Christmas. That was what he needed. Not Molly alone in the dark and the snow, and definitely not those slippery, lacy, barely there knickers too close to his fingers. He needed the family environment – anything to keep reminding him that Molly could never be anything more than a sister.

Not unless he wanted to lose the closest thing he'd had to a home since his parents died.

-

Molly stared after Jake as he followed her mum inside.

"Now, you have to try my latest batch of mince pies. Can you believe, I have fifteen different sorts of mincemeat to try this year? You'll have to keep track and tell me which one you like best," Philippa said, as they disappeared into the hall and through the doorway on the left that led to the lounge.

Jake might be in the house, but he wasn't home. Not really. *He still doesn't believe he belongs here.* Which was pathologically stupid.

He'd stood stiff and uncertain, even as Philippa had thrown

her arms around him, welcoming him home. After all these years, shouldn't he know better? Unless… unless this was her fault. Unless her lingerie and talking about kissing had made him awkward around her family.

She could kind of understand that, she supposed. Even if it was still stupid.

Well. One thing she could do this week, possibly even while persuading him into bed with her, was make it clear that this was his home now, as much as it was hers. That's how it worked. Like the half starved stray cats mum took in, Jake was theirs now. And nothing he could do would change that.

Not even sleeping with her. Probably.

As long as they didn't get caught.

Molly shut the door behind her as she followed Tim inside. A plan formed in her mind, even as the mulled wine scented air warmed her. Dumping her case at the bottom of the stairs, she headed directly for the kitchen – or more specifically, the pan on the stove, her brain still whirring.

Jake wanted this, as much as she did; she was almost certain. What if he hadn't been avoiding her for the past year out of embarrassment for her, or because he didn't want her trying to hit on him again? What if it was because he wanted it too, but didn't think he could let himself have it?

In which case, if she just explained everything, explained about her resolution, how it just needed to be a one-time thing – something to get it out of their systems so she could go back to London and sleep with other men… Okay, maybe she wouldn't put it quite like that. But the basic idea was good.

They'd have one stolen night together, and nobody else ever needed to know. Especially not her family. Hell, it wasn't like she'd told anyone about last New Year, was it? So he had to know he could trust her to keep their secret.

All she needed was one night. And Jake, from what Tim had told her about their university days, and what she'd guessed from his revolving door of sleek brunettes in the past, was the king of one-night stands.

Dipping the ladle into the pan of mulled wine, Molly poured a healthy portion into one of the glass mugs her dad always brought out on the first day of December. Then she added a little more.

"That for me?" Tim leant a little too heavily against the kitchen counter as he asked, so Molly shook her head.

"I don't think anyone can handle Dad's mulled wine after a night on cinnamon vodka in the George and Dragon," she told him.

"Ha!" Tim helped himself to a mug, and held a hand out for the ladle.

Molly rolled her eyes and handed it over. "It's your hangover."

"I'm a big boy. I can handle it." He eyed her over the pan of spiced wine. "And speaking of not taking on more than you can handle—"

"Which we weren't," Molly pointed out. She had a very bad feeling about where this conversation was going.

"About Jake." Tim didn't look drunk anymore. Molly knew that just made him more dangerous.

"Also not what we were talking about."

"It is now." Pausing to take a sip of his mulled wine, Tim raised his eyebrows at her expectantly.

He was waiting for her to break. She knew that technique from years of being the youngest. He thought all he needed to do was act like he knew something already and she'd give up all her secrets.

It was a shame for him that she'd grown up.

"Actually," Molly said, schooling her face into a concerned expression. "I did want to talk to you about Jake, in fact."

Tim's jaw tightened. "Look, Moll. Jake's a good bloke. But—"

"I know he is," Molly interrupted quickly. The last thing she needed was Tim warning Jake away from her because he'd got the, well, right idea.

"That's why it's so sad he still doesn't feel at home here, don't you think?"

"He…" Tim blinked. "What?"

"Didn't you see him? He was hanging back when we arrived, didn't hug Mum properly… we're the only family he's got, and he still doesn't really feel at home here. It's sad." Time to pull out the puppy dog eyes. "You should talk to him. Make him understand that we really do want him to be here."

"I should… yeah, no. That's not going to happen." Tim shook his head emphatically.

"Then maybe I should," Molly said, trying to sound virtuous. "I mean, it *is* Christmas. Goodwill to all men and so on."

"Just how much 'goodwill' are you intending on giving him? That's what I'm worried about." Damn. Maybe her brother wasn't quite as drunk as she'd assumed, if he could still leap to these conclusions on minimal evidence. Well, minimal evidence and some ridiculously slinky lingerie.

"Look, Jake's like a brother to me, right?" Molly said, eyes wide and hopefully innocent looking.

"You're much nicer to him than you are to me," Tim pointed out.

"I'm nicer to Great Aunt Mabel than I am to you, and God knows she doesn't deserve it." Molly sighed, and changed the subject, hoping Tim wouldn't notice. "Is it our turn to have her this year, by the way?"

"Mad Mabel? No, the cousins have her for the festivities. She'll be here for New Year, though. She hasn't gotten over having to miss last year's and not meeting The American."

"Lucas," Molly corrected automatically, but her mind was already filling with memories from last New Year's Eve. It was as if they just hovered around the edges of her mind, all the time, just waiting for the slightest reason to flood back and consume her. Hearing the song that had been playing downstairs when Jake kissed her, even if she was standing in the middle of a crowded supermarket, still made her feel like she was back in his arms. The smell of cinnamon had been playing havoc with her brain for weeks. And as for actually seeing him again… God, Jenna was right. She really needed to get him out of her system if she ever wanted to be able to think about another man the same way.

But first, she needed her brother to stop looking at her with such suspicion.

"I'm going to go take my bag up to my room," she said, taking one last glug of mulled wine. *Mmm, cinnamon…*

Tim grabbed her arm as she put her glass down. "Wait, Moll. Listen. About Jake…"

"Tim, you really don't need to worry—"

"But I do. Because you're my little sister. And Jake…" Tim took a deep breath. "Look, he's my best friend. And I don't know what you two were talking about when I banged on the car window, and I'm going to pretend I never saw the… stuff that fell out of your suitcase. But just in case you were getting any ideas – ideas that I absolutely do not want to know about, by the way. Jake's a good guy. The best friend you could want. He's a part of this family. But he is one hundred per cent *not* the guy for you. Okay?"

When was the last time she saw her brother looking so serious? Gran's funeral, maybe? Either way, he meant what he said – which made Molly wonder how much of the drunkenness outside the pub had been an act, a trick to pretend he hadn't noticed the intense way she and Jake were staring into each other's eyes.

With a deep breath, Molly placed her hand over her brother's, looked him in the eye, and lied.

"Tim. Jake is like a brother to me. Trust me, he'd probably be as disturbed by this conversation as I am. There's absolutely nothing between us. Okay?"

"Okay." But Tim's gaze never left hers, as though he was searching for a chink in her lie. Then he sighed, and stepped back. "He's a good bloke, Moll, don't get me wrong. But he's not right for you. Hell, for a start, you don't know where he's been, if you know what I mean." Oh, she knew. Jake's revolving door of women was legendary. And now probably wasn't the time to mention to Tim that one of the places Jake had been was up her shirt.

Tim sighed. "He's just not good enough for you," he said, the words heavy, and Molly realised she actually had to answer him. More than that, she needed to reassure him.

"Not something you need to worry about." She shifted uncomfortably, from one foot to the other. She should argue, should tell Tim he was wrong, she should defend Jake. But she couldn't, because then he'd know for sure. "Jake and me? It's the most ridiculous idea I've heard all year."

She grinned up at him, one last determined lie, and kept her smile in place through sheer force of will as she spotted Jake, standing in the doorway behind Tim, a plate of mince pies in his hands. His face was rigid, his mouth fixed in a straight line, his eyebrows low. Oh God. How long had he been there? How much had he heard?

And worst, how much did he hate her right now?

# Chapter 6

*"He's just not good enough for you."*

The words made Jake slam to a halt outside the kitchen, almost losing a mince pie or two from the plate he was carrying in the process. They shouldn't, though. It wasn't as if they weren't expected.

Hell, if he had a little sister, he wouldn't let a guy like himself date her – especially not one five years older. And if Molly brought home some London loser who gave even a hint of being like him – or Tim, for that matter – Jake would intimidate the guy all the way back down south in a heartbeat.

Molly deserved the best – someone without baggage, or issues, or an unfortunate history with women.

And she clearly thought so too, from her response – or else, she was busy putting her brother off the trail. In which case, what the hell did she imagine would happen if they *did* get together? Tim would be mad as hell with him for daring to touch her, and furious with Molly for lying to him. The worst of both worlds.

Staring down at the mince pies, their little pastry holly leaves promising the perfect Christmas that everyone knew was impossible in reality, Jake mentally cursed Philippa Mackenzie and her powers of persuasion that had convinced him to stay with them for the holidays. If he'd had any sense, any will power, any brains, he'd have insisted on staying at home and just driven over to the Mackenzie house for Christmas Day itself, just like he'd done every other year.

Instead, he'd let Philippa talk him into an extended stay, imprisoning himself in the house with the one woman he couldn't touch, however much she seemed to want him to, and regardless of how long he'd fantasised about it. Even better, he'd got to hear his best friend hold forth on why he was a lousy human.

Merry Christmas, Jake.

He glanced up again and saw that Molly had spotted him. Too late to pretend he wasn't there, or even that he hadn't heard anything. From her horrified expression, she knew exactly what he'd heard.

"Mince pie, anyone?" Jake held up the plate, a little icing sugar cascading over the side. "Your mum thought you might need it to help soak up the mulled wine."

"Good plan, man." Tim grinned as he grabbed a pie from the plate, sending crumbs flying as he bit into the pastry. He, at least, didn't seem to realise how long Jake had been standing behind him. That was something, Jake supposed. Although he wasn't sure what, exactly.

God, what a mess.

"What on earth are you three still doing in here?" Philippa appeared behind him, and he almost bit his tongue trying not to jump. "I sent Jake in here ages ago to fetch you through!"

Tim paused halfway through biting into the remains of his mince pie, his gaze flying to Jake's. Jake stared back blankly, not willing to give anything away – especially in front of Tim's mother and sister. His best friend's thoughts on his history with women wasn't exactly a surprise, and they'd deal with it later – if they had to at all. 'Dealing with it' would probably include an excess of vodka and not actually mentioning it, which was absolutely fine with Jake, but probably best done away from the Mackenzie family home.

In fact, Jake almost looked forward to it. It sounded… normal. And a hell of a lot less terrifying than nine days resisting the charms of Molly Mackenzie.

"We're just coming through now, Mum." Molly gave Philippa a cheery smile that looked utterly false to Jake, then turned to ladle another spoonful of mulled wine into her glass. Nice to see that they were all dealing with the tensions of the holiday season in time tested, adult style – with alcohol and denial.

If only he could remember where Glen Mackenzie hid the good whiskey…

"Come on then!" Philippa ushered them all along, and Jake found himself carrying the stupid plate of mince pies back through to the lounge where he'd started. Halfway through the door, Philippa squeaked, "Oh!" and piled a few extra pies onto the plate from a tin on the edge of the counter.

Perfect. Because if Jake had to endure a family evening with the Mackenzies tonight, he was going to need all the stodge he could get to soak up the required quantity of alcohol.

As if reading his mind, Tim called back, "Bring some more mulled wine, Moll?" and she nodded.

At least they were all on the same page in one area – even if they were miles apart in everything else right now.

The lounge sparkled with the twinkle of fairy lights, strung across the fireplace, and wrapped around the otherwise bare tree.

"Where are the decorations?" Molly frowned as she sat down on the end of the sofa closest to the tree. Jake waited until she was settled before he chose his own seat – on the opposite sofa, as far away from her as possible. It meant he was uncomfortably close to the fake flames leaping in the electric fire, but it was a sacrifice he was willing to make.

"Oh, I didn't want to decorate the tree without any of you here to help me," Philippa said, sitting beside him. "Too depressing. I thought the five of you could do it tomorrow. We'll put some Christmas music on, eat mince pies, it'll be fun."

"Five?" Jake asked, frowning. Surely she wasn't counting him in this.

"Of course! You and Tim and Molly and Dory and Lucas. If they ever get here." Her gaze flashed nervously to the clock on the mantelpiece. Jake knew she hated it when Glen was out late in the cab, especially in bad weather.

"Have you heard anything from Dad?" Molly asked, obviously following the same train of thought.

Philippa shook her head. "Not for a while. He texted to say he was at the airport and their flight was delayed. Nothing since. He's probably in the coffee shop with a good book, knowing him."

"He'll call before he leaves, I'm sure," Jake said. Philippa took his hand absently and patted it, almost as if he were one of her own children.

Jake pulled it back before the moment could go on too long.

"You're right," Philippa said. "And I know that Dory won't miss the chance to decorate the tree, so I'm sure she'll be here soon enough, snow or no snow."

Jake had to admit, that did sound like Dory. And if she and Lucas were there, they definitely wouldn't need him. "Unfortunately, I'm going to have to beg off," he said, trying to sound regretful. "I have an important client meeting tomorrow."

"On Christmas Eve?" Philippa sounded scandalized at the very idea of anyone working so close to the big day.

"Afraid so. But I'm sure the others will do a great job."

"Nonsense," Philippa said in what even Jake recognised as her 'don't argue with me' voice. "What time is your meeting?"

"Uh, eleven?"

She nodded. "Perfect. You can all get up early and decorate the tree before you leave."

Tim groaned, but across the room Molly had a small smile on her face, as though she was pleased he would be forced to endure every aspect of a Mackenzie family Christmas. Or was it just her incredibly tempting company she wanted to torment him with, knowing he couldn't do a damn thing about it?

*Little tease.* Just the thought made his mouth dry. He needed to get out of here, quick. Mulled wine really wasn't cutting it anymore.

"Well, if we're having an early start, I'd better get to bed." Jake got to his feet, ignoring the way Molly's eyes widened with dismay. "Thank you for the mince pies, Philippa, and I hope Glen is home soon. If you'll excuse me? I assume Tim and I are in the attic as usual…?"

Philippa bounced up from her seat, the perfect hostess, her short, greying auburn curls settling around her head again like a halo. "Of course. You must all be tired! Well, apart from Tim." She looked critically at her middle child. "But I suspect bed might be good for you, too. Go on, all of you. Off to bed. Big day tomorrow!" She shooed them towards the door with her hands, and Jake couldn't help but remember being eleven years old and being chased out of Mrs Mackenzie's kitchen when he and Tim were trying to steal biscuits.

Tim slung an arm around Jake's shoulder, almost like an apology. "Come on, then. We've been told." He lowered his voice to a murmur. "Besides, I've got Dad's second best whiskey hidden up there."

Jake faked a smile. Maybe that would take his mind off Molly in bed a floor below him, but he doubted it.

Molly Mackenzie and her soft skin, her bright hair, and her bag full of silky lingerie had taken over his brain, and he was damned if he knew how to get her out of there.

But he knew he had to try.

—

Molly lingered behind as the boys made their way up the stairs towards the attic room their dad had converted for Tim the minute he hit puberty. With two sisters sharing the room beside him, and a mother who didn't much believe in knocking, he had declared that a teenage boy deserved some privacy.

Molly had spent years wondering what Tim, Jake, and their other friends talked about or did up there in his private den, but she'd never wanted to sneak up there as much as she did tonight. Especially if she could get Tim out of the way…

"Your bed's all made up too," her mum said. "Go on. I'll clear up down here."

"Are you sure?" Molly paused in the doorway. "I can wait up with you for Dad and Dory, if you like?"

But her mum shook her head. "Who knows how long they'll be. No, I'm going to make one last batch of mince pies, in case they're hungry when they get in, and then I'm going to bed with an audio book. You go on up. Get some rest. You're looking too pale."

"Okay." Leaning over, Molly kissed her mum on the cheek and turned to climb the stairs. Sleep would be good. It had been a long day – a long six months, really.

"It's so good to have you home," Mum said, wrapping her arms around her waist for a moment."

"It's really, really good to be here." Molly smiled. However crazy everything else was, at least home was always home. "Night, Mum."

Upstairs, Molly flipped on the light switch and looked around the bedroom she'd shared with Dory throughout their childhood, until her sister left for university. Small pink flowers still covered one wall, dotted with bare patches where the wallpaper had been torn away when removing posters or artwork, over the years. Now, just the twin beds with their rosebud covers remained, bedside tables between them, and two desks-cum-dressing tables against the far wall.

Why had no one ever thought to change it? Dory hadn't lived at home in years. Of course, once Molly had finished university and come home herself, she'd moved into the spare room, with its queen sized bed and non-floral decoration. It had made sense, as the only one of them still living at home at the time. Even once Tim had rebounded from his job in Edinburgh that summer, he'd just moved back up into the attic while waiting for the next big thing to come along.

The little pink room she'd grown up in hadn't been needed anymore. Until Dory came home with a surprise guest in the form of Lucas, last year, and Molly had been ousted back to the children's zone.

Molly flopped down onto the bed nearest the window, her case on the other bed, and stared up at the ceiling as if she could see through to where Jake was sleeping if she only looked hard enough.

She wasn't a child any more. Hadn't she proved that, getting a new job two hundred miles away and moving to the capital, all on her own? So why did she always feel like one, the moment she stepped into this room?

Even Tim treated her like the baby, still. Warning her off unsuitable men, when she could have been sleeping with anyone in London for the last six months. Okay, she *hadn't*, but she could have done, and he would never have known.

She sighed. But even that wasn't as bad as Jake. So desperate to keep her firmly in 'best friend's sister' territory that he couldn't even admit that if they hadn't been interrupted last year, things could have been… phenomenal. That was the only word for it.

With a yawn, Molly forced herself to sit up, and rifle through her case for her pyjamas. Mum was right. She needed sleep if she wanted to be on form for tomorrow – and she did.

After all, she only had eight days left to meet Jenna's challenge and show Jake once and for all she wasn't a child anymore.

# Chapter 7

**CHRISTMAS EVE**

Despite her best intentions, Molly slept poorly. It didn't help that every time she shifted in her sleep, some part of her would knock up against the wall, or bang into the bedside table. How had she ever slept in a bed so narrow?

And, of course, once she was awake it was impossible not to think about Jake, asleep just one floor above her. Was he asleep, though? Or was he tormented by thoughts of her, too?

At least he had a proper bed. He and Tim had apparently tossed a coin weeks ago, to see who would get the double and who would have the sofa bed, and Jake had won three times in a row. Even Tim had given up then.

As the illuminated numbers on the alarm clock clicked over to 5.35, the front door slammed and Molly jerked upright. Downstairs, she heard people shushing each other, as if that would make a difference now. Honestly. Never mind sleep – it clearly wasn't happening anyway. It was Christmas Eve and it sounded like her dad and sister were home.

Jumping out of bed, she padded out of her room towards the stairs, not switching on any lights in case anyone else had managed to sleep through Dory's not-so-stealthy entrance. Besides, who needed light? She knew this house inside out and backwards. She could find her way around in the dark when blind drunk and half asleep, and still avoid the creaky floorboards on the stairs. God knew she'd had enough practise in her teenage years.

Except… "*Ooof.*" Molly froze. There wasn't usually a wall of warm muscle and flesh between her room and the stairs. As she crashed into it, strong arms wrapped around her waist to keep her upright.

"Molly?" Jake's warm whisper was somehow less of a question, more an incredulous complaint.

She pulled back, just enough to look up at him, but his arms stayed exactly where they were. Molly really wasn't objecting. Her breasts almost brushed against his chest, driving her crazy.

"Morning," she whispered back, although forming words in her suddenly dry mouth took a lot more effort than usual. Her eyes had adjusted to the darkness and, even with only the faint light of a streetlamp outside the landing window, she could still make out the lines of his face. Of course, it helped that they were standing mere millimetres apart. So close, she could feel the warmth of him through the thin fabric of her pyjamas. "Couldn't sleep?"

He shook his head. "I thought I heard your dad get home. Thought I'd go and welcome everyone."

"Same here." She gave him a half smile, not even sure if he could see it. "Plus, you know, mince pies for breakfast."

"Yeah. Of course."

They should move. Dad and Dory and Lucas would be coming upstairs at any moment, and running into her and Jake having a moment on the landing probably wasn't how any of them wanted to start their Christmas holiday. But how could she pull away, when she finally had Jake exactly where she wanted him?

Molly licked her lips, and Jake made a tiny sound in the back of his throat that hit her straight in the libido. "Jake…"

"Yeah. I know." His jaw was so tight the words came out clipped. Taking a chance, Molly shifted the mere millimetres it took to press her body up against his, sighing in relief as she felt him against her. If she'd ever needed proof that he wanted this as badly as her, she had it, pushing against her stomach right now.

Stretching up on tiptoes, she trailed her fingers up from his chest to his neck, pulling his lips down to meet hers. For a moment, she felt resistance in the muscles of his throat, but in the space of a heartbeat it was gone, and she was finally, finally kissing Jake Sommers again…

Somewhere, a floorboard creaked.

Jake tore himself from her in a moment, and Molly stumbled back against the wall, her heart beating too fast for her to count, as the landing light flickered on.

Across the hallway, Jake's eyes were wild, wanting, and he was gripping onto the banister rail with white knuckled hands. His hair looked messier than Molly could ever remember it being. Had she just done that? Or was it just the result of a night spent tossing and turning?

She needed to say something. To address what had happened between them, to ask what happened next. But there were already footsteps on the stairs, and it was too late.

"Hey, guys." Lucas blinked at them as he lowered his suitcase onto the top step, his eyes red and tired. "Sorry, did we wake you?"

Molly shook her head, stumbling over words in her brain before they could even reach her lips.

Fortunately, Jake had more composure than her. "I thought I heard something, but don't worry. I'm an early riser."

"And I… couldn't sleep." Molly managed. "Are Dad and Dory downstairs?"

Lucas nodded. "And already getting stuck into the mince pies. Me, I need a little sleep before I can face any more merriment. It's been a long couple days. See you in a few hours? I've got something I need to talk to you about actually, but…"

"Sleep first." Molly smiled, and let Lucas pass to get to the guest room. "We'll save you a mince pie. Probably."

As Lucas's door shut behind him, Molly stared across at Jake again.

"We'd better get downstairs," he murmured.

She wanted to object. Wanted to insist that they figured this out at last. But any moment now, she knew Dory might come up or Tim might emerge from the attic. It wasn't the time or the place.

"Okay. But… we'll talk? Soon?"

"Sure," Jake said.

Molly sighed. Maybe she'd believe him more if he wasn't already halfway down the stairs, getting away from her as fast as possible.

Looked like she still had some work to do. But she smiled as she followed him downstairs. At least she knew now that his body was willing. And clearly, things like this were going to keep happening until they got it out of their systems. Really, the only logical thing to do was sleep together and get it over with.

All Molly needed to do now was appeal to Jake's common sense. How hard could that be?

He was an idiot. Devoid of any sense at all. If he'd had the slightest smidgen of intelligence, he'd have ignored the sound of the front door in the early hours and stayed in bed, safely away from the temptations of Molly Mackenzie, until it was time to leave for his meeting.

But he hadn't. And so now he was sitting at the kitchen table with Molly, her sister and her father, all eating mince pies with cups of tea for breakfast – and he couldn't get the scent of her, let alone the feel of her body against his, out of his head.

She smelt like vanilla. He'd thought maybe it was just the mince pies or the mulled wine, the night before, but even in the early morning, with her auburn hair wild around her pale face, and wearing the most ridiculous robin pyjamas he'd ever seen, she still had that sweet, warm smell about her.

Jake risked a glance at Molly across the table, laughing at something Dory had said. She leant forward for another mince pie and the neck of her red top gaped slightly, giving him a perfect glimpse of creamy curves.

Actually, he was quite fond of the pyjamas, if he was honest.

Dory wiped pastry crumbs from her mouth. "Right. I'm going to go wake Tim up so we can get on with decorating this tree. If we're lucky, we can get the whole thing done before Mum gets up – and before the jet lag catches up with me and I crash out."

Glen Mackenzie shook his head at his eldest daughter's energy. "Well I, for one, am going to follow Lucas's example and get some shut eye before all hell breaks loose later today." Standing, he shook his head. "Christmas Eve. I swear, it's more exhausting than the day itself."

"And we need you on form for mulled wine making, Dad," Molly said, grinning. "You know that's the only reason so many people stop by."

Glen smiled back. "Extra mince pies for you." Pressing a kiss to the top of her head, he wrapped an arm round Dory's shoulders as she headed for the door, stopping her. "It's so good to have both my girls home again."

As Dory and Glen headed up the stairs, Jake tried very hard to look anywhere except at Molly. Something that proved rather more difficult when she stood, moving to perch herself on the edge of the kitchen table right beside him.

"Dory will be back with Tim any moment," he pointed out, wishing he could move his chair back without feeling like an utter coward.

"Then we'd better talk quickly, hadn't we?"

Jake sighed. She always had been persistent. "Look, Moll—"

"Don't call me that," she interrupted.

"I've always called you that."

"You called me that when I was a kid." She frowned. "In case it's escaped your notice, I grew up."

"Trust me. It really, really hasn't." How could it, when he'd been pressed so damn close to every inch of her very grown up curves, had felt them against every part of him. And she had to be aware of exactly how his body had reacted to them, too.

He wanted her. Jake was man enough to admit that. He wanted Molly Mackenzie in a way he hadn't wanted anyone in a long time.

But life was rarely as simple as just getting what you wanted. Even when it was being served up to you in robin themed pyjamas.

"So. We kissed. Again." Molly raised her eyebrows expectantly.

"I noticed."

"Seems to keep happening."

"Twice in one year doesn't really count as—"

"Jake." Her voice was mild but serious.

Jake sighed. "Yeah. Okay. I know."

"So? What do you suggest we do about it?"

Oh, he had plenty of suggestions. Most of them involved a bed, but to be honest, at this point he wasn't really all that picky. Up against the wall of the landing, the back seat of his car, hell, he'd take her anywhere he could get her.

Except… this was Tim's baby sister. Glen Mackenzie's little girl. And he couldn't touch her.

"Molly, we can't. You know we can't. It would tear up your whole family." And almost certainly get him quickly and efficiently exiled from the only family he had.

"Only if they found out," Molly said with, he felt, rather undue optimism.

At least she was admitting the basic problem, he supposed. "I heard what Tim said last night."

"Yeah, I figured." With a sigh, she sank down off the table and onto the chair beside him. "And what I said too."

"I did." *It's the most ridiculous idea I've heard all year.* Her mocking laugh hadn't faded one bit in his memory. "And you were right. It's ridiculous."

"It didn't feel ridiculous upstairs." And wasn't that just the hell of it? Molly inched her chair closer. "It felt right."

"But that doesn't mean it *is* right." Jake leant back in his chair, gaining a couple of inches between them as Molly sighed.

"Do you really believe that?" she asked, and Jake bit back on the instinctive, immediate urge to say, *no!*

"*Deck the halls with boughs of holly!*" Tim's voice echoed through the darkened hallway, followed by Dory's answering, "Shh!"

"Fa la la la la, you two," Tim added, leaning in the doorway to the kitchen. Did he look suspicious or just half asleep? Jake honestly couldn't tell anymore. "Apparently we've got a tree to decorate. You coming?"

"Of course!" Molly leapt to her feet and headed for the lounge, without even glancing back at Jake. Which should have been a good thing but somehow it wasn't.

"I'm gonna need coffee for this. You in? The tree thing, I mean." Tim asked, halfway through a yawn, as if it were a natural thing that Jake be there, decorating the Mackenzie Christmas tree. As if he were just another one of the Mackenzie siblings.

But he wasn't, and he could never forget that.

"Yeah." He stood up, tried to give his best friend a convincing smile. "I'm in."

# Chapter 8

Dory had already pulled all the boxes of decorations out from behind the sofa where their mum had hidden them, and Molly squealed with excitement as she saw her favourite decoration sitting half unwrapped from its tissue paper, on the top of the first box. With gentle fingers she picked it up and let it spin, the delicate coloured glass beads glinting in the fairy lights.

"Is that the one I bought Mum from that school trip to France?" Tim asked, appearing with a cup of coffee in hand. "Can't believe that hasn't been broken yet."

"No," Dory said, peering at it. "Yours was green and gold. That's the one Jake bought."

"What did I do now?" Just the sound of Jake's voice from the doorway made Molly's insides tighten. God, she was in trouble.

"Bought this bauble." She turned to hold up the delicately wrought wire framed bauble, each strand of it strung with red and white glass beads that left the perfect circle swirling with colour as it turned in the light. "Although how either of you got them home without bending or breaking them amazes me."

Tim, Molly knew, had bought Mum hers purely in the hope that she'd forget how much trouble he was in for getting caught smoking on that trip. He'd been fifteen, and not really the most thoughtful of boys, so he hadn't brought anything for the rest of them.

Molly had been ten, and cross that she didn't get a present, so Jake had given her his bauble – presumably bought for his own mother for the same reasons. She could still remember the way her heart beat faster when he'd placed the box in her hands, silver tissue paper poking out of the top.

Maybe she'd been wrong, when she told Jenna she'd never thought of Jake that way until after last New Year's Eve. Perhaps he'd never seemed like a real possibility, but the moment he'd handed her that box... her little pre-teen heart had definitely fluttered.

She half expected Jake to come closer, to look at it with her, for them to share a moment with the memory. But instead, he just nodded over his cup of coffee and stayed firmly in the doorway – practically outside. "So I did."

Molly turned to face the tree so the others didn't catch her scowl, and hung the bauble front and centre. "There. I declare the great Mackenzie early morning tree decorating session open."

"Then let's get to it." Dory appeared at her side with decorations hanging from each of her fingers, and Molly raced back to the box to choose her own.

It was always the same, every year – a competition to see who could find the best, most prized decorations and give them pride of place. Dory, Molly could see, already had the tiny wooden nativity scene, and the pompom robin, and Tim was rooting around in the boxes already. Which meant she'd have to be quick if she wanted to find the jingling Santa or the sequin Christmas tree – and not get stuck with the job lot of glass icicles Mum had bought a few years ago.

Molly paused, her hand already inside the box, as she spotted Jake still leaning against the doorway. "I thought you were helping."

"You three seem to have it all under control," Jake said, one eyebrow lifted.

But that wasn't the point, Molly wanted to say. He wasn't holding back because they didn't need him. He was staying out of it because he felt he didn't belong. And that was stupid.

Especially if he thought he didn't deserve to be part of the family because he'd been feeling her up on the landing less than an hour ago.

Pulling out the next decoration, Molly unwrapped the tissue paper to find another of her absolute favourites. This one, a glittering silver star, had been brought back from a family holiday donkeys years ago and, to be honest, was starting to look a little worse for wear. But it wouldn't be Christmas without it.

Standing up, she handed it to Jake, who stared at it with confusion.

"You're supposed to put it on the tree," Molly said, helpfully.

"Where does it go?" Jake asked.

Molly shrugged. "Wherever you want it to. It's your tree too, remember."

His gaze met hers at that, and the longing there touched her even deeper than the wanting had earlier. Being part of her family mattered to him – so much that he was willing to deny everything that was between them to make sure he still had a place here by the end of the holidays.

Was it unfair of her to ask him to risk that, just for one night with her? Almost certainly.

But as Molly watched Jake hang the silver star, hidden slightly on one side of the tree, she couldn't help but feel it was an inevitability. If Jake wanted to belong here, they had to move past the insane attraction that was driving them both crazy, one way or another.

And Molly could only think of one way.

Jake tried not to watch as Molly stretched up to place the angel on the top of the tree, but given the way her top rode up providing him with a glimpse of her smooth white skin above her pyjama clad bottom, he couldn't help himself. Besides, he'd just hung countless glass icicles all over the damn tree. Didn't he deserve some sort of reward?

Feeling eyes on his back, he glanced round and found Tim watching him. Damn. Caught. Jake looked down at his watch in a feeble attempt to pretend he hadn't just been caught ogling his best friend's baby sister. Still only just eight thirty. He had hours until he could legitimately get away to his meeting, and a horrible feeling that tree decorating wasn't the end of the family activities he'd be expected to take part in today.

He sighed, and settled down onto the sofa. The others could finish up. It wasn't like it was really his family tree anyway.

Previous years had been so much easier. He'd just pitched up after he clocked off work on Christmas Eve and headed straight down to the pub with Tim. Christmas Day itself was a walk in the park compared to all the festive preparations he appeared to be required to take part in this year. Presents, food, booze, Doctor Who, some board game or other, bed. Then straight home again on Boxing Day. Barely thirty-six hours of pseudo-family fun. Easy.

Molly dropped onto the sofa cushion beside him, bringing a cinnamon and pine scented breeze with her. "See? Wasn't that fun?"

"Masses," Jake lied. Tucking her bare feet up under her, Molly turned to look at him, and he tried not to shift uncomfortably under her gaze. "What?"

"I'm sorry. I never thought to ask before. But… do you have decorations from your family you'd like to add to the tree?"

Jake blinked in surprise, suddenly very aware that Tim and Dory were being a little too obvious about not listening to not actually be eavesdropping.

"Uh, no. Not really."

"Because we wouldn't mind," Molly went on, earnestly. "I mean, this is your Christmas tree too. Your family celebrations."

Except it wasn't, and they both knew it. "Honestly, Moll, there's nothing."

"Surely there must have been something? Or are they all on your tree at home? Maybe next year, you can take a look through and pick a few to bring with you?" Why did she have to push things?

Always too far, too fast, and usually at the worst possible time.

"I don't have any of my parents' decorations any more," he admitted, and watched Molly's expression struggle through disbelief to disappointment to confusion.

"You don't… why?"

"I need more coffee," Dory announced suddenly, apropos of nothing. "Come on, Tim."

"What?" Tim looked utterly bemused as his big sister dragged him out of the lounge. Jake gave thanks that at least one member of the Mackenzie family knew when something was none of their damn business. Maybe she could teach her little sister.

Molly settled down a little closer to him, bringing her knees up to her chest so her bare toes pressed against his thighs. Her toenails were painted deep red with tiny silver stars on them. He stared at them for a moment too long before looking away, suddenly swamped with the feeling that the colour of her toenails was weirdly a too personal thing to know about her.

Which, considering he'd had his hands up her top earlier that morning, was completely ridiculous.

"Why didn't you keep any of your parents' Christmas decorations, Jake?" Molly asked the question in a softer voice, this time, but it didn't make him want to answer it any more.

"They weren't… Christmas with my family wasn't like the way your family does Christmas, Moll."

"Molly," she corrected, obviously unable to stop herself even when she was trying to be sensitive or nice, or whatever the hell it was she was doing. "How do you mean? Were they… I mean, your parents always seemed really nice."

"They were," he said simply. "They were good people, who loved me. And I loved them very much, too. But… you might not realise this, Molly, but not everyone feels the same way about Christmas as you guys do."

Molly's wide eyes neatly conveyed her complete incomprehension of his words. Jake sighed.

"Look, if my parents were still alive today, this is what would happen. I'd come home on Christmas Eve, after work. My mum would have decorated the house in whatever this year's colour scheme was, so it looked good for dinner party guests over the holidays, or whatever. I'd have dinner with them, then come over here to grab Tim and go to the pub. Christmas morning we'd have breakfast, open presents, then sit around reading or whatever while Mum cooked Christmas lunch, because she hated having anyone else in the kitchen while she cooked. After dinner, maybe we'd watch a film, then head to bed. And I'd leave to go home again first thing Boxing Day. It would be nice, and we'd enjoy seeing each other, but it wouldn't be the highlight of any of our years. Whereas here..."

"Christmas matters," Molly said, emphasis heavy on the second word. "It's the best part of our year."

"Right." Jake didn't want to admit that, in lots of ways, it had become one of the best parts of his, too, since he started spending it with Molly's family.

"Is that why you didn't keep any of the decorations? Because they didn't mean anything?" She sounded honestly curious, like she really wanted to understand him, his life. Hell, she'd only known him since she was born.

But this... this was something new. And the shift made him uncomfortable.

"Mum changed them every year," he said with a shrug, wishing she'd just drop the subject. "There was nothing of sentimental value there, so there didn't seem much point keeping them. When I sold the house, most of their stuff I boxed up to sell or give away. I kept the stuff that had mattered to them, or that had important memories for me."

"That makes sense." Molly's eyebrows furrowed over her pale green eyes, and he wondered if she was any closer to fathoming whatever riddle she thought he presented. "But... what do you put on your tree at home now, then?"

Ah. Jake had a feeling she really wasn't going to understand this one. "I don't have a tree. Didn't seem like there was much point, since I'm here the whole time anyway."

"This year, yes. But most years you're only here for forty eight hours or less."

"Plenty of time to do Christmas." He sighed as her face fell again. "Molly, please. I love spending Christmas with your family. I'm honoured to be part of your celebrations. But once it's done… I'm usually ready to get back to work, to be honest."

"I get that," she said, although her tone made it clear she thought he was crazy. "But the thing is, Jake… if this is your family Christmas, why do you keep reminding everyone that you're not part of the family?"

Did he? "Well, it's the truth."

Molly shook her head. "Not to us, it isn't." Getting to her feet, she held out a hand to him and pulled him up. "Come on. Let's go see where they've got to with that coffee. You're going to need caffeine before you head to your meeting."

"True." After a night of barely sleeping, plus a morning of resisting – or not – Molly's many temptations, he'd take all the help he could get to get through the rest of the day.

"And then, when you get back, we still need to finish our talk," she added, already halfway to the door.

Jake groaned. *That* was definitely going to take more than coffee.

# Chapter 9

Christmas Eve always made Molly feel like a child again. The anticipation, the excitement, the friends and family dropping by with gifts and cards, or just to sample Mum's mince pies. But this year, as she dressed in her favourite red tartan mini kilt and a black sweater with a robin on it, she couldn't help but wonder how weird it must have been for Jake, coming from a family who didn't make a big deal of Christmas, to try and fit in with their excess of holiday spirit.

He liked it, she was almost sure. He just still wasn't sure if he was really allowed to be a part of it.

Running a comb through her hair, Molly braided it away from her face, tucking it into a messy bun at the back, then reached for her make up bag. She wanted to look good today, especially if she might be able to get Jake alone to finish their conversation. Still, she couldn't help but smile at the knowledge that not only had he wanted her in the dark, unable to see her at all, but he'd had his eyes on her all morning despite her Christmas pyjamas, wild hair and no makeup.

The poor guy didn't stand a chance.

Downstairs, Jake had left early for his meeting, apparently via the supermarket for a last minute chocolate orange emergency dash on behalf of her mother. Dory and Lucas were in the lounge,

56

adding one last decoration to the tree – a vintage glass bauble Dory had looked *very* surprised to see in Lucas's hand. Tim was hiding in the attic with his laptop, which Molly thought was probably the best place for him, but it left her at a bit of a loss as to what to do. In previous years she'd have been working Christmas Eve, and often Christmas Day itself. All this holiday time was a luxury she wasn't used to. She supposed she should spend the time wrapping presents, but instead she headed into the kitchen to find her parents.

Her dad was stirring a pan on the stove, the heady scent of spices and alcohol rising up in the steam.

"Mulled wine at eleven o'clock on Christmas Eve morning?" Molly perched on the edge of the kitchen table. "What is the neighbourhood coming to?"

"Oh, hush, you." Dad flashed her a quick smile. "It's for later. For the guests. Your mum wants to get in and make more mince pies, so I thought I'd get this batch made up now. We can reheat it later."

"Bet you need to taste it first though, right?" Molly teased.

"Of course!" her dad sounded insulted she'd even ask. "I couldn't serve sub-par mulled wine to any visitors now, could I?'

"Is that nearly done, Glen?" her mum asked, bustling into the kitchen from the hall. "I've got another five sorts of mincemeat I want to try out today. Ooh, Molly, since you're not busy, you can help me."

For a second, Molly contemplated claiming she had something very important to be doing elsewhere, but in truth, a morning spent up to her elbows in pastry with her mum didn't sound all that bad.

"I'll grab my apron," she said, and slipped off the table to the hook behind the door.

"Great." Was that surprise in her mother's voice? Molly turned round just in time to see her parents exchanging a look. What did that mean? She supposed that most years she might have begged off the baking, but this year… okay, she'd been a little homesick the last six months. It was nice to have some time with her mum, that was all.

For the first three batches of mince pies, they worked mostly in silence, or singing along to the Christmas tunes on the radio. But, just as Molly dug out the fourth sort of mincemeat – suet free cranberry and apple, apparently – Philippa turned down the music.

"So, how's London?" she asked.

Molly froze, jar of mincemeat in hand. How *was* London?

Her mum had asked the question with the deliberate nonchalance Molly remembered from her teenage years – the sort that tended to indicate that she already knew the answer and was just waiting for Molly to decide whether to tell the truth or lie.

She hated those questions.

"It's fine," she said, placing the jar on the counter next to where her mum was rolling out the pastry. "You know. Busy. Always something fun going on."

Apparently, anyway. Other than after work drinks with the same people she saw all day, Molly hadn't really had much time or energy for seeing the sights or the bright lights. Her flatmates – all of whom had been living together for over a year before she came along – had their own lives. Boyfriends, friends, fancy jobs and big nights out. Most evenings Molly just curled up with a bowl of pasta on the sofa and caught up on the telly.

"And how's the job?" her mum pressed. "I must say, it's nice not to have you working over the holidays for once."

It *was* nice. Except… part of her missed the buzz of being part of the hotel family, all stuck together making the best of the situation as Christmas parties got out of hand, or the chef ran out of sprouts, or whatever. The huge office she now worked in, even with its open plan layout and 'town hall' company meetings, just didn't have the same feel of comradeship. Not even when they were out doing karaoke.

"The job's fine too," she said, finally. "I mean, it's kind of weird to just be sitting in front of a computer most days. But the people are nice. And I've made some really good friends."

Well, one friend. Jenna. Unless you counted Stefan from accounts, which Molly still most definitely did *not*.

"That's good." Philippa handed her a double-sided cutter, and Molly began cutting out rounds of pastry for the bottoms of the pies, while her mum got on with greasing the trays. "I did worry…"

"Worry about what?" Molly tried not to snap but, really, when were they all going to get over the idea that she was the helpless baby of the family? They'd let Dory go off to New York on her own without a moment's concern, hadn't they?

"Well, that you might be a little bit… lonely, I suppose." Her mum gave her a half smile as she pushed the tray towards her. "You have so many friends here, plus your career at the hotel… it was a bit of a surprise when you suddenly decided to leave. I worried that maybe we'd done something to make you want to go."

Molly's heart felt too big for her chest. "No. Of course you didn't." She wrapped her arms around her mum in a floury hug. "How could you think that?"

"You just seemed so happy with your life here until, suddenly, you weren't. We just didn't understand what had changed."

What *had* changed? What had made this year the year she'd fulfilled that vague, annual resolution of getting out, moving on, finding a new life somewhere else?

Molly bit the inside of her cheek, very afraid she knew the answer. She'd wanted to prove something. To Dory, with her perfect life. And to Jake, who'd pushed her away and avoided her for a whole year, the idiot. And to herself, she supposed. To prove that she could get what she wanted as much as the next person, even when it had felt like she couldn't.

But she hadn't ever wanted to upset her parents.

"Nothing had changed, Mum," she promised, not even sure if it was a lie. "I'd had 'move to London' on my hopes and dreams list for years, you had to know that. God knows I talked about it often enough!"

"Don't blaspheme at Christmas," her mum snapped, on reflex. Molly hid her smile behind her hand. As a once a year churchgoer who was letting her eldest daughter live in sin with an American, most of the year the odd slip like that would pass completely unnoticed. But at Christmas, Philippa's religious heritage tended to come back in force – if not enough to actually make her do more than attend the midnight mass at the local church. "And yes, you talked about it. We just…"

"Never thought I'd do anything about it," Molly finished for her. "Of course not." Why would they? She was the child who never finished anything. Her mother had files of childhood mementos for all of them. While Dory's was filled with merit certificates and glowing reports, and Tim's with photos of complex models and computer competition wins, hers had mostly half finished paintings and stories that only lasted half a page. She was the daughter who took two years of driving lessons but never quite got around to putting in for her test. The one who switched A Level subjects twice before the end of her first year of sixth form. The one who never brought the same boy home twice.

She was, officially, a flake. And to think Tim was more worried about Jake's history of one-night stands! At least he'd managed to pursue an actual career *and* stick at his training long enough to start it. The best she had to offer the world of consistency and dependability was seven years working on and off at one hotel – even if she'd had six different jobs there during that time.

"It's not that we thought you *couldn't*, love," her mum stressed. "It was just…"

"You never thought I'd get things together long enough to do it. I understand." Molly shook her head and stepped away, reaching for another jar of mincemeat just for something to do. "But I did. I got myself that job, found myself that flat, and made myself a new life. All by myself."

"Yes, you did," her mum said firmly. "And we are incredibly proud of you, you know that?"

That feeling was back in her chest. The one that made her feel like her heart might burst. "You are?" The words came out small, and Philippa smiled.

"Of course we are. You decided you wanted something, set out to get it and you did it, all by yourself." She brought a hand up to cup Molly's cheek, then flapped at it to try and remove the flour she'd left behind. "But that doesn't mean you can't decide you want something else, if it turns out it's not right for you. You can always come home again. Okay?"

Molly nodded, her throat tight. Yes, she knew there would always be a place for her here, if she needed it. But taking it would mean not following through on yet another thing in her life. It would mean giving up. Everything she'd worked for, every bit of credibility she'd gained, would be lost.

She'd be flaky Molly, living at home again, back at the hotel – if she could even get another job there.

And did she even *want* to leave London? The job was okay, her flat was reasonable, and she had friends. Okay, she had a friend. And all she had back in Liverpool was her family, friends she'd known her whole life, a community she felt part of, a job she loved and… Jake, living just an hour away and popping in whenever he was on their side of town for meetings.

Could she go back to that life, if she wanted to? No, probably not. God, how would she cope with seeing Jake over the family dinner table every other Sunday, tucking into his roast dinner and pretending that he'd never kissed her, never wanted her in the way she wanted him? Badly, she'd bet.

No. The safest plan was the one she'd come home with. Seduce Jake, fulfil her resolution and get this crazy lust out of her system. Then she could get back to building the life she'd dreamt of in London.

Who knew? Maybe she'd even have a new man to bring home with her next Christmas.

# Chapter 10

Jake was beginning to suspect that there wasn't a single Terry's Chocolate Orange left in the whole of Merseyside.

It had sounded like a simple request when Philippa had whispered it to him on his way out the door that morning. Pick up five chocolate oranges on his way home. How hard could that be?

Seven supermarkets and three corner shops later, Jake had his answer. Very.

Wham! blared out of the speakers of the last disappointing shop, singing about last Christmas, and Jake slammed the door behind him to get away from it. He'd finally escaped the ever present reminder of what he'd done last December, in the form of Molly Mackenzie and her robin pyjamas. He didn't need George Michael reminding him that he was an awful person.

Okay. Christmas was just going to have to be Christmas without chocolate oranges. He was almost certain that the Mackenzie family would get over it. One day.

Either way, he'd stalled long enough. He'd dragged his meeting out so long his clients had felt obliged to offer him five cups of tea, then he'd swung by the office to see if he could clear up some issues with a colleague, only to discover he wasn't in. It was Christmas Eve, his secretary had told Jake, with faint censure in her eyes. He was home with his family.

The *where you should be* went unspoken.

So, he was on his way back to the closest thing he had, anyway. With Toblerones instead of oranges, because they had the Christmassy packets with snow on the peaks. Best he could do.

The Mackenzie driveway was already full when he arrived, as was the street immediately outside, so Jake found himself parking around the corner in a hidden alley. As he approached the front door it opened before he even had a chance to knock.

"Jakey!" A woman with a bright purple streak in her dark hair launched herself into his arms without warning. "It's been forever!"

It had been, by Jake's estimation, almost exactly a year. The only time they ever tended to see each other was Christmas Eve. "Hello, Lara," he said, disentangling himself from Molly's best friend. "How's the mulled wine?"

"Scrummy." She flashed him a grin. "As is Molly today, in that little kilt of hers…"

Jake suppressed a groan. *Of course* Molly had told Lara. And so *of course* she was going to use it to make his life hell.

Fantastic.

"Who else is here?" he asked, making his way through towards the kitchen.

"Everybody!" Lara said, voice vibrating with glee and festive cheer.

"Great." Just what he needed today.

Christmas Eve at the Mackenzies' tended to be quite the event – another reason he usually showed up later, if he could. Last year, Molly and Lara had joined him and Tim in the pub after hours of mulled wine with various relatives and friends.

It had been a late start, last Christmas Day.

Still, last Christmas was the last time he'd been able to look at Molly without her knowing how he felt about her. Without seeing the glint in her eye that told him he could have what he wanted – or at least, what she thought he wanted.

She was wrong. But there was no way he was explaining why

to her.

Molly had her new life now, the one she'd been talking about for years – and it was down in London. The last thing he wanted was to jeopardise that for her by starting something together when he'd always be two hundred miles away.

No, actually, the last thing he wanted was to finally get one perfect night with her – then watch her go back to her regularly scheduled existence without another thought for him. To have to endure next Christmas, and the one after that, hearing about her new boyfriend or her brilliant life that he wasn't a part of.

Or, even worse, have that night found out and lose any access to the only family he had at all.

"Jake, you're back! Lovely." Philippa patted his arm, leaving a small smudge of flour on his jacket sleeve, then lowered her voice. "Did you manage to get the… things we discussed?"

He shook his head, and handed her the carrier bag full of Toblerone. "Not a sign of one, I'm afraid. But I got the next best thing."

Philippa peered into the bag. "They'll have to do, I suppose. I just can't believe I forgot to buy them sooner! Thank you, anyway." Dory appeared from the lounge, and Philippa shoved the bag behind her back, eyes suddenly wide. "Lara, why don't you come through and grab a plate of mince pies to offer round in the lounge. I've got a new batch of mulled wine mincemeat ones…" Keeping the bag of Toblerone out of sight at all times, she bustled back towards the kitchen, Lara and Jake following.

"What's with all the mince pies this year?" Lara whispered as they both were handed plates of pastry topped treats.

"No idea," Jake murmured back. "But there's been a hell of a lot of them."

"The ones with the pastry stars on the top are the mulled wine mincemeat ones, and the lattice topped ones are apple and cinnamon mincemeat." Philippa pointed to each plate in turn, then ushered them back through towards the lounge.

Jake wondered if he might be allowed to take off his coat at some point. It was kind of hot inside.

"I know Mummy Phil is always a bit… manic about Christmas," Lara said, picking off a pastry star and eating it. "But does she seem a little excessive even for her to you this year?"

"I went to ten different shops looking for chocolate oranges for her this afternoon," Jake admitted. "She was very clear about their importance."

"Weird." She took a bite of the mulled wine mince pie. "As are these."

The lounge was packed with people, all with mulled wine glasses in hand. Molly looked up from where she sat on a floor cushion, surrounded by a few other friends that Jake vaguely recognised. She smiled up at him, and he gripped his plate of mince pies a little tighter. It was all very well telling himself that one night with her would be worse than never having her at all, but how was he supposed to keep on believing that when she smiled that way?

She'd pinned her gorgeous auburn hair away from her face, intricate braids holding it out of her way, save a few loose waves around the front that made her eyes look wider and greener, somehow. Her slender legs were crossed, the tiny red and black skirt she was wearing riding up enough to give him a great look at them through thick black tights.

Lara was wrong. She didn't look scrummy. She looked irresistible. Which was going to be a problem.

"You're back," she said, smiling up at him. "How was your meeting?"

Meeting. There had been a meeting, somewhere before the chocolate orange fiasco. "Um, long. And tedious." Mostly because he'd stayed long enough to let the clients change their minds about what they wanted another dozen times. If he hadn't been avoiding Molly, he'd have been in and out in under an hour.

"Have a seat." Molly gestured to the cushion beside him, and Jake took a step back instinctively.

"I have to hand these round for your mum," he explained, even though Lara had happily plonked herself down on the arm of the sofa and was eating her way through her plate of mince pies. She caught him looking at her mid mouthful.

"They grow on you," she explained, which wasn't really the point.

Dory and Lucas were on the other sofa, talking with old family friends Jake recognised vaguely but couldn't name. Glen was in his armchair, chatting with one of his taxi buddies. Everybody already had a plate with a mince pie on it.

"Seriously, what is with the mince pies this year?" He hadn't meant the comment to be heard, but Glen's smile showed it had been.

"You know my Philippa," Glen said. "She likes Christmas to be perfect."

"Best day of the year," Dory agreed. "Every year."

"And this year... well. She has more reason than ever to make it memorable," Glen continued.

"What reasons?" Molly asked, a frown line appearing between her brows.

"All her children home with her, to start with." Glen reached for another mince pie from Jake's plate. "And all of them scattering to the four winds on January second. She wants to make this year something special."

"Christmas is always special here," Jake said. His eye caught on the star he'd hung on the Christmas tree. Maybe he needed to stop feeling like an outsider, and just be grateful he'd been let in at all.

On January second, Dory and Lucas would go back to New York. Molly would catch the train to London, and Tim would head off to Switzerland to start his new job. With none of them at home, Jake would have no reason to stop by for Sunday lunch, or even just a cup of tea if he was passing.

They might not even all come home for Christmas next year at all. Which meant there'd be no place for him, either.

He'd spent so much time worrying about being forced out of the family for sleeping with Molly, it hadn't even occurred to him that with Tim moving away now too, there might not be a place for him anyway. Oh, he was sure he'd still stop by with a courtesy Christmas card and a bottle of wine or something, sometime over Christmas week. Have a glass of mulled wine and a mince pie before he headed home on his own.

God, he might even have to buy a tree.

Was Glen trying to let him down gently, give him the hint that things would no longer be the same, after this year? And if so… he might never really see Molly again, not like this. Not a whole week living in the same house, enjoying each other's company, being a family.

He may never get another opportunity to be close to her, if nothing else.

Maybe the worst thing wouldn't be to have her once and then have to go back to just being her friend. Maybe the worst thing would be never seeing her again, and knowing he'd missed his only shot with her.

Jake took a bite of mince pie and glanced casually over at where Molly was chatting again with her friends. She looked happy. Vibrant, alive, and happy. She'd found what she wanted in life, and he wouldn't be the one to take that away from her.

But if this was his last Christmas with the Mackenzie family, he damn well intended to make it memorable, too.

# Chapter 11

Something had changed. Molly wasn't sure what, exactly, but it had. Jake hadn't taken his eyes off her all afternoon. She could feel him watching her as she said goodbye to her friends, made plans to meet them in the pub later. Even Lara had confirmed that she wasn't imagining it when Molly had texted her, moments after her best friend left the house.

*It's the mini kilt,* Lara had texted back, not entirely helpfully. After all, Molly knew full well that Jake was attracted to her. She just couldn't figure out what had encouraged him to accept and enjoy that.

Or how far he planned to take it.

By the time all their guests had headed on their merry way, and they'd had their traditional Christmas Eve dinner of Tesco frozen canapés cooked by the tray load and more mince pies, it was time for church.

Molly didn't go every year – in fact, she hadn't been for quite a few. For the past few years, when the midnight service was actually at midnight she'd usually been in the pub if she wasn't working. This year, however, the service had been moved to nine thirty, which sounded a lot more manageable. Of course, she wasn't sure any of them should be allowed near the advent candle, given the sheer quantity of brandy in the mulled wine, but otherwise she

68

was actually looking forward to it.

Maybe she was more homesick than she'd been ready to admit to her mum.

"Your coat, milady." Jake held out her duffel coat for her to slip her arms in, wrapping it around her to keep her warm. For a moment, she closed her eyes and relaxed into his embrace, letting herself imagine how it would feel to do that without all those pesky clothes between them.

Then she heard her dad clearing his throat in the doorway and her eyes flew open again.

"Everybody ready?" Glen asked, and Molly nodded.

"Think so. Come on, we can save everyone seats if we leave now."

The midnight service was the one time of year that church was filled to capacity, according to Auntie Susan, who was rather better than the 'every Sunday' part of church going than the rest of them. She waved cheerfully from the row of pews third from the front, and they made their way forward to join her. She'd kept them the whole pew, but by the time everyone had crammed in, Molly found herself pressed closer to Jake than she'd expected him to be comfortable with.

But, to her surprise, he simply let his arm rest along the back of the seats behind her, and allowed his thigh to press up against hers as if it were perfectly normal for them to be so close.

Molly had to admit; it felt normal.

In fact, she thought as she stood for the first carol, it felt more than normal. Sharing a carol sheet with Jake, hearing his low voice singing *Once in Royal David's City* softly by her ear, being there with him and her entire family… it felt right. Every bit as right as it felt when he kissed her, or when she was wrapped up in his arms.

God, she was in trouble.

*Molly Mackenzie, don't you blaspheme at Christmas!* Her mother's voice was so sharp in her mind that Molly had to glance across to make sure Philippa hadn't actually read her mind and chastised her out loud.

Some days, she wouldn't put it past her mum. Especially if she'd been able to telepathically tell what Molly had been imagining while Jake's leg was pressed against her thigh. *Very* inappropriate for church.

The service seemed to go on forever, but Molly suspected that was only because she was so desperate to get Jake alone and talk to him. As they finally finished up the closing carol, she turned to him, ready to try and articulate in whispers and facial expressions the need for them to get alone and fast.

"Right. Pub," Tim said, grabbing Jake's arm and effectively destroying all of Molly's plans. A crowded pub filled with her siblings was *not* where she wanted to have this conversation.

Still, it couldn't be any harder than having it at home with Mum knocking on the door asking if they wanted mince pies every five minutes, right?

With a sigh, Molly followed Tim, Jake, Dory and Lucas out of the church, back into the snow, reminding herself that it was still only Christmas Eve. Technically, she had until New Year's Eve to figure all this out with Jake.

Except she was pretty sure she'd go crazy if she didn't get him alone before then.

Jake sucked in the cold winter air and tried to find some sense of calm and balance. Or, at the very least, some way to forget how short Molly's skirt was, and how good her body felt next to his. As much as he wanted to just drag her off to some hotel room somewhere, that wasn't on the cards for tonight. Instead, he had the rest of the evening in the pub with her brother and sister, followed by a whole day with her parents tomorrow.

Sex was very firmly off the cards.

But somehow, that was almost all right with him. If this were to be his last Christmas with the Mackenzies, he wanted to enjoy it. Tomorrow, he'd talk to Molly about the possibility of something more – maybe they could even escape to his house for a day or so between Christmas and New Year. He could claim he was working, she could say she was visiting friends…

And they'd both still be lying to people they cared about. But what was the alternative? Get caught screwing in her childhood bedroom by her father? No thank you. Jake had moved past that level of risk and humiliation almost a decade ago.

But if he didn't find some way to have her before the holidays were over, there was a fair chance he was going to lose his mind.

The pub was conveniently situated across the road from the church, and already packed with people leaving the service by the time they got across. Dory, Lucas and Tim grabbed the last free table, while Molly somehow wound up at the bar with him – something he suspected was the result of planning rather than chance.

"What am I buying?" Jake asked, as he jockeyed for position at the bar.

Molly leant against him, stretching up on her tiptoes to put her mouth near his ear as she answered. "Three pints, a gin and tonic and a glass of white wine." Jake tried not to shiver as her breath brushed across his skin.

"Pints of anything in particular?"

She shrugged, and the movement made the robin on her jumper bounce. There was absolutely no way that should be attractive. Except… he knew exactly what was under that sweater. Had explored the territory early that morning. And God, he wanted to again…

"Tim said you know what he wants, and Lucas said he'd try whatever you were having."

Easy enough. Jake forced himself to focus on getting the barman's attention, not on the way Molly had leant back against the bar, her elbows resting on its polished surface as she surveyed the pub.

"You know, no one can see us here. I mean, no one we know.

They're all hidden behind that pillar over there. And they definitely can't hear us. So if there was something you wanted to say – or do – now might be a really good time…"

The woman was temptation incarnate.

"I have too many things I want to say to you to get them out in between drinks orders." If he just didn't look at her, maybe he'd be all right.

Except then she shifted, turning to face him, one elbow still on the bar and her chin in her hand, looking up at him from under thick, long lashes.

"Which just leaves us with something we could do…"

Damn it. No man had enough willpower to resist this. Certainly not him, with his registered weakness for everything Molly Mackenzie.

He risked a quick glance over his shoulder, but she was right; there was no way anyone they knew could see them. Which didn't mean this was a good idea, but it *did* mean he'd run out of arguments against it. Even to himself.

Swearing under his breath, Jake grabbed her waist and yanked her closer to him, his mouth finding hers more on instinct than through aim. His body had known what it needed to do for months now – it was only his brain getting in the way.

Her lips were sweetly parted ready for him, and she gave out a tiny sigh as they sank into the kiss. It sounded like relief, which Jake could understand. Something inside him had been winding up, tighter and tighter, all year now. And this kiss, this decision, released just an iota of that tension.

It would be back, he knew. This was only a temporary fix. One kiss would never be enough.

Regretfully, Jake pulled back, although his fingers stayed clutching the fabric at her hip as she let out a whimper of disappointment. He rested his forehead against hers, just for a moment. Just long enough to whisper, "I know. I know," and have her understand that everything she felt, he felt too.

"We really do need to talk," she murmured back, and Jake nodded, even as he stepped back. He couldn't look away from those wide eyes, though.

"Later," he promised.

She pulled a face, but agreed. "Tell me one thing, though?"

One thing. How hard could that be? "Sure."

"What changed today?"

He didn't bother pretending he didn't know what she meant. What had changed today? Every assumption he had about the future. About his place in a family that could never really be his.

But most of all, he'd realised that pretending he didn't want the only thing he'd ever wanted with such furious passion was a waste of time.

He smiled, an apologetic, gentle smile, he hoped. "Everything."

Her answering smile was warm. "I know exactly what you mean."

# Chapter 12

**CHRISTMAS DAY**

Ever since she was a little girl, Molly had never been able to sleep on Christmas Eve. Long after Tim let slip that Father Christmas wasn't real, even into the years where she'd stumbled into bed from the pub ages after her stocking had been filled and left on the end of her bed, there was something about the anticipation of the day to come that left her staring at the ceiling for hours after she turned in.

This year, it all seemed a thousand times worse.

Not only did she have the joys of Christmas Day to look forward to, but Jake had finally promised her a proper conversation about their... situation. Which meant she had to figure out what she actually wanted to say.

*Jake, I made this resolution, and then my friend challenged me, so I kind of have to sleep with you before New Year. Then I'm back off to London and you don't have to see me again until next Christmas. Okay?*

Somehow, she wasn't quite sure that was going to cut it. Which was weird because, a week ago, that kind of proposition was *exactly* the sort she thought Jake would like. No emotions, no strings, just one night of fun.

Okay, so how about…

*Jake, I'm going insane because I can't stop thinking about what it would be like to have you. Give me one night, and I'll make damn sure it's the best one either of us have ever had.*

Except, while she sure that would be the case for her, Jake had considerably more experience in bedroom activities, from what she could tell. How the hell could she make that promise to him? He'd laugh her out of the bedroom.

So, maybe…

*Jake, I'm sorry, I forgot to get you a Christmas present this year. But I've thought of a way to make it up to you…*

Turning over, Molly buried her groan in her pillow. This was impossible.

And the worst thing was, all these scenarios anticipated her being alone with Jake at some point tomorrow, and being able to do anything about the ridiculous levels of sexual tension they had now reached. When, in truth, they'd be spending the day opening presents with her family, peeling carrots and watching Doctor Who.

It was Christmas. She had to focus on her family, not her libido.

And for the first time, that felt like a real sacrifice.

As always, she must have slept eventually – although not before she heard her bedroom door creak open and felt the familiar weight of a fully laden stocking laid on her feet. But when she had closed her eyes to hide the fact she was awake from her dad, she must have actually dropped off because the next thing she knew, Tim was screaming, "It's CHRISTMAS!" from the top of the attic stairs and playing Slade at full volume.

Molly checked her clock. Seven thirty. That was a lot better than some years.

Rubbing at her eyes, she grabbed her stocking and headed down to the kitchen in search of coffee.

"You're up early," she said, smiling as she watched Jake make coffee in the dim light of the under cabinet lamps.

He turned and, leaving the coffee half made, stepped towards her, heat in his eyes. Molly swallowed. This really was a different Jake to just a few days ago.

"Merry Christmas, Molly," he murmured, his lips barely milli-metres away from hers.

"The others—" He cut her off with a kiss, and the warmth of his arms around her made her forget whatever she'd been about to say anyway. God, she could kiss this man for hours…

The creak from the stairs behind her barely registered with Molly, but by the time Dory entered the kitchen Jake was already back by the kettle, stirring mugs of coffee ready to hand out.

Molly blinked, and dropped to sit in one of the kitchen chairs, her stocking full of presents at her feet.

"Where's Tim?" Dory asked, looking between them with what Molly hoped wasn't suspicion as she leant her stocking against the kitchen cupboards. What had gotten into Jake? The pub the night before was one thing, but right there in the kitchen with the family about to descend?

"I think he disappeared into the bathroom." Jake handed Dory a mug of coffee. "After ensuring that none of us were ever going to get any more sleep."

"Apart from your mother," Glen announced. "She still has her earplugs in so slumbers on, oblivious."

"Lucky lady." Lucas appeared behind him, stocking hanging from one hand. Dory handed over her mug with a sympathetic smile.

"Jet lag getting you down, Lucas?" Molly asked.

"I don't think we can hold the jet lag entirely responsible for this one." Lucas took a long gulp of coffee. "Although if there are any more of those little pies around that might help…"

"I think we can help with that." Dory pulled the lid off the large cake tin in the middle of the kitchen table and doled out a lattice topped mince pie. "Probably until the end of time," she added, staring at the ridiculous quantity of mince pies still remaining.

"What are you all doing in here?" Tim asked, appearing in the

doorway with his iPod speakers in one hand, now playing *Rockin'
Around the Christmas Tree*, and his filled stocking in the other. "We
have to open the stockings around the tree. You know this, people!"

"Just getting some caffeine first." Molly held up her mug.
"Besides, Mum's still asleep."

"Not anymore she isn't." Tim gave a wicked grin, then disappeared into the lounge, obviously expecting them to follow.

Molly glanced back at Jake as the others made their way through.
"Where's your stocking?"

"I left it upstairs, I think."

Oh, honestly. "You know the rules, Jake. Tell me you didn't
open it already?"

"I wouldn't dare. But, can I just say, it's kind of creepy hearing
your dad sneak into the bedroom and leave it on my bed."

"It's not creepy," Molly said, rolling her eyes at him. "It's festive
and nice. Besides, it wasn't Dad, it was Santa."

"I think that might be even worse." He smiled, a private sort
of smile she knew he wouldn't risk giving her if anyone else were
in the room. "Besides, I don't need to open it. I already got what
I wanted most for Christmas."

She raised her eyebrows. "Really?" Because in that case, he really
wasn't wishing hard enough.

"I got to kiss you." Jake shrugged. "I'm happy."

Molly stared after him as he sauntered out still sipping on his
coffee. She was starting to think this One Night With Jake idea
wasn't at all what she thought it was. And she knew for certain
that she was very, very out of her depth.

With a deep breath, she picked up her stocking and followed, just
in time to see Jake disappearing upstairs to fetch his own stocking.
She wanted to go after him, to finally get him alone in a room
with a bed, but her family was waiting. For a moment she stood,
undecided, just inside the kitchen doorway where, apparently, her
brother and sister couldn't see her, as she suddenly realised they
were talking about her.

Next to the front door, just beside the door to the lounge, Tim and Dory stood with their heads close together. They were keeping their voices low, but if Molly concentrated she could make out enough words to follow the gist of the conversation.

"I'm just not sure it's a good idea," Dory said, frowning. "You know how Molly is."

Molly tensed at the sound of her name, ducking a little further back into the kitchen just in case either of them looked over.

"Don't worry," Tim replied. "I've already spoken with her. Told her that he's not her type."

"Like that would ever stop her! Come on, Tim. Tell Molly she can't do something and you *know* she's going to go right out and try." Molly bit the inside of her cheek to stop herself arguing back. Honestly. They made it sound like she hadn't grown up any more since the age of twelve.

"Yeah, maybe," Tim conceded, and Molly seriously considered taking his present back. "I was kind of drunk and not really thinking it through."

"Tim!" Dory sounded despairing. Good.

"But it's okay! Turns out that Jake was listening in."

"How is that better?" Dory asked. "Poor Jake. He'll think it's something to do with him."

"Well it is, kind of. And anyway, all that matters is that if Jake thinks we're against the idea, there's no way he'll let anything happen with our baby sister." What she wouldn't give to slap the smug look right off her brother's face. "Problem sorted."

Dory didn't look entirely convinced, which surprised Molly. She'd have bought Tim's logic herself, if it hadn't been for the kiss in the kitchen that morning.

"Except Jake probably believes that we think he isn't good enough for her. You know how he likes to rise to a challenge… and he's always wanted so badly to be a part of this family."

"You think he'd seduce Molly just to prove a point?"

"I think he'd fall into a relationship with her if it meant he knew for sure he'd get invited back here every year."

"That's ridiculous!" Tim said, louder than he probably meant to. Dory shushed him, and he dropped his voice as he continued, "Jake's always invited here. He knows that."

Except he didn't.

Molly's head thunked back against the doorframe. Suddenly Jake's change of attitude made a little too much sense. He was trying to buy himself a permanent place in the family. She wanted one night only, and he was after forever – but not for her, not really. Because he wanted to be a Mackenzie.

God, this was such a mess.

"Look, Tim, talk to him," Dory pleaded, and Molly forced herself to pay attention again. "Explain things. That we love him, that he *is* part of our family, whatever happens. But that Molly is finally getting her life together, moving to London and everything, and we just don't want a fling with him to jeopardise that."

"Yeah… those really aren't the sort of conversations I have with Jake," Tim said.

"Fine. I'll tell him, then," Dory said.

"Great." Tim paused, not moving away but not talking.

"What?" Dory asked, and Molly leant just a little bit closer to be sure of hearing.

"Do you really think Molly's got things together in London? That she's… well, happy?"

*Of course I am,* Molly thought, just as Dory said, "Of course she is! She's wanted to move away for years, you know that. And that job at the hotel… she's far too bright to have stayed there. She's in a new city, with a great job, new friends—"

"No, Dory," Tim interrupted softly. "That's you. That's what you wanted."

Dory stared at him. "Molly wanted it too."

"Are you sure?"

As her brother and sister stared at each other in silence, Tim's words echoed in Molly's head. *Are you sure?*

Was she? Right then, it was hard to be sure of anything at all. Least of all what the hell she was doing with Jake.

# Chapter 13

Present giving in the Mackenzie household always started with the opening of stockings around the tree, while everyone waited for the coffee to take effect. By the time Jake made it downstairs with his stocking, the others were already knee deep in wrapping paper.

"I told them they should wait," Philippa said as he took the spare seat left for him on the sofa beside her. "But you know how they are."

"I do." Jake smiled softly across at Molly, unwrapping a fortune telling fish by the tree, but she didn't return it.

Not a good sign. Had he spooked her, kissing her that morning?

"And thank you," he added to Philippa, indicating his stocking. "You didn't have to."

Philippa's eyes grew wide. "Nothing to do with me, you know that. It's all down to Father Christmas."

"Of course." Jake wondered if by the time Philippa could be persuaded to drop the act for her children, Dory and Lucas would have provided her with some grandchildren to keep it up for. He rather hoped so.

His stocking was filled with the usual assortment of small gifts. A new comb, a paperback Glen had been raving about, a small tub of multivitamins he took as a hint from Philippa that he was looking tired, shower gel, festive socks, his own fortune telling fish and one of the Toblerones he'd bought as a substitute for the usual chocolate oranges.

"Right, fish at the ready everyone!" The fortune telling fish were a tradition all of their own. Tim ripped open his own packet and placed the filmy red fish in his palm. His sisters followed suit and, after a moment and some prodding from Dory, so did Lucas and Jake.

"Aw, moving head and tail!" Dory kissed her boyfriend soundly as the fish in his palm wiggled at both ends. "I knew you loved me."

"I tell you often enough," Lucas murmured, kissing her back. "Figures you'd trust some fish over me."

"Are those sides curling?" Tim asked, staring at his own fish. "Apparently I'm fickle."

"We could have told you that," Molly teased.

"Me? Fickle? What did you get, then?" Tim asked. "If I'm fickle, whatever you are must be beyond even the might of the fortune telling fish."

Jake looked at the fish in Molly's hand as she stuck out her tongue. It had curled up completely into a little circle of red film. *Passionate*, his mind filled in, the instructions still in front of him. Well, the fish was on form this year.

Glancing down at his own fish, Jake watched as the head and tail both moved. *In love.*

He crumpled it within his fist. What did a red plastic fish know anyway?

After the stockings came the real gifts. Jake relaxed a little as they handed them round. He'd had this one sussed for years now. All he needed to do was send Philippa an email in early November asking what everyone wanted, and she'd send back a carefully thought out list with a selection of options for each family member. As long as he didn't deviate from the list, he was fine.

He tensed as Molly reached for her gift from him. In all the ups and downs of the last two days, he'd almost forgotten that he *had* deviated from the list this year. Just once.

"To Molly, love Jake," she read out the label. Beside him, Philippa raised her eyebrows, obviously very aware that the tiny box Molly held couldn't possibly contain the DVD box set she'd suggested. "Thank you!"

"You haven't opened it yet," Jake pointed out.

Molly tore off the wrapping paper with unashamed glee, revealing the small, flat, velvet box inside. Jake very carefully ignored the looks Dory and Tim were exchanging across the room.

Perhaps this hadn't been his best idea ever. But when he'd bought it, he'd assumed that he and Molly would spend the entire holiday being awkward around each other, and that a nice present might go a way to helping them be friends again.

Besides, when he'd seen it in the display case, he'd known it was perfect for her, and he just couldn't resist.

Molly opened the box slowly, and let out a little squeak. "I love it!" She beamed at him and he knew, without her having to say, that she wanted nothing more than to thank him properly, but couldn't. Not with everyone watching.

"Let me see." Dory elbowed past Tim to get a look at Molly's present. "Oooh, that's gorgeous!"

"Help me put it on?" Molly asked, and Dory took the delicate silver chain and wrapped it around Molly's wrist. As she fastened it, the tiny snowflake charm that hung from it sparkled in the fairy lights from the tree.

"Very nice work, Mr Sommers," Philippa whispered. "Much better than a DVD."

Jake shifted uncomfortably in his seat, suddenly aware that Tim and Glen were both watching him with matching looks of interest – and suspicion.

Yeah, definitely not his best ever idea.

–

"He bought you jewellery, Moll." Dory handed her a pair of fluffy red mittens. "Don't tell me that's nothing."

Molly shrugged as she pulled her mittens on, trying not to stare at the tiny snowflake dangling from her wrist. It was perfect. How had he known?

"You know Jake. He likes to make an effort with presents." Inspiration struck. "You know, I think he asks Mum for help. Maybe she suggested it."

Dory didn't look convinced. "He bought me a book."

"Yeah, but a book you really, really wanted."

"True," Dory conceded.

"And anyway, I think he was trying to make it up to me for missing my moving to London party. Or something." *Stop digging, Molly.* She was rapidly approaching protesting-too-much territory.

Dory paused, halfway through wrapping a pale blue scarf with a knitted rendition of the Snowman around her neck. "You know you can talk to me, right? If there's anything…"

"There's nothing for you to worry about with me and Jake." It wasn't *quite* a lie, Molly decided. After all, Dory would be heading back to New York in a week or so. Whatever fallout there was from this holiday, she wouldn't have to worry about it.

"Fine. But I mean other stuff too. If you're unhappy in London—"

"Why would I be unhappy?"

"Maybe you're lonely." Dory gave her a half smile. "I know I was, when I first got to New York. But it got better."

"Of course it did! You met Lucas. And his crazy but crazy-rich family."

"*Anyway,*" Dory said, dragging them back on track. "You can talk to me. If you need to. That's all I wanted to say."

"Okay." Molly knew she wouldn't take her sister up on the offer – admitting all her failings to her perfect sister? Not a fun way to spend the holidays – but it was still nice to know she was there. "Now, come on. We have a snowman to build!"

The veg was all peeled, the wrapping paper tidied away, and

the house still littered with presents. The turkey was in the oven, Dad was having a nap and Mum was reading her new book in between dealing with dinner, so the rest of them had been kicked out into the snow like troublesome children.

Well, actually the going outside part had been Tim's idea.

"I got it!" Tim announced proudly, brandishing a large carrot overhead. "She never even noticed."

Molly had a suspicion that her ever-organised mother had bought the carrot with this very eventuality in mind. It looked far too much like the perfect snowman nose to be eaten with dinner.

Outside, Lucas and Jake were deep in conversation. Molly flashed a suspicious look at Dory. Had her sister asked Lucas to talk with him? And if so, what about? But if anything, Dory looked even more suspicious.

Since when had Christmas Day involved so much secrecy?

"When was the last time we built a snowman?" Tim packed snow tightly between his hands until he had the perfect ball.

"Last time it snowed at Christmas, I guess." Bending down, Dory began sifting through the snow on the patio to find perfect stones for the eyes.

Tim began rolling his snowball through the fresh white powder, building it up to snowman body size. "Molly, you do the head?"

Nodding, she grabbed a handful of snow herself, carefully shaping it. But before she could roll it, temptation overtook her.

"Ow!" Tim looked up and glared as she scored a perfect hit on his arse. As he scooped up snow to retaliate, Molly ran for cover behind the first suitable object she saw. Which just happened to be Jake.

As snowballs pelted them, Jake turned to wrap his arms around her waist and lifted her off the ground, striding towards the end of the garden and the shelter of the rhododendron bushes.

"Us against them?" Molly asked, breathless, as Jake began lobbing snowballs back over the bushes. A shriek suggested he'd hit Dory rather than Tim.

"Looks like it." Jake's gaze locked with hers and Molly forgot all about the snowballs landing harmlessly around them. "That okay with you?"

Molly bit her lip. "I think I can handle it," she said, but the way her breath caught at the words betrayed her doubt. Hell, she didn't even know what she was trying to handle. A one-night stand had seemed like the limits of her options, but all of a sudden she had a snowflake bracelet and Jake looking at her like he might kiss her again, right here behind Dad's prize rhododendrons, and not give a damn who caught them.

"So do I." Jake's voice was warm, and Molly knew instinctively that he wasn't talking about himself. He believed that *she* could handle it, even though he had to know she hadn't got a clue what *it* was.

It didn't matter because he had faith in her.

And that meant the world.

—

Another snowball flew over the bushes and landed smack between them on the ground. Molly scrambled to grab it, add a little snow and toss it back. This time there was a manly yelp from Lucas. Jake had to admit, the girl had great aim.

"Hey, what were you and Lucas talking about before?" Molly asked as she gathered more snow. "Dory looked very suspicious."

Jake chuckled. "She should. That guy has plans."

"What sort of plans?" Molly pestered, sounding more like her twelve-year-old little sister self than she had for a while. He'd almost forgotten how much she hated not knowing everything.

"You'll have to wait until after dinner to find out." Jake tossed another snowball out, and responded to Tim's latest jibe with the sort of language he wouldn't want Philippa hearing.

"Dinner's hours away," Molly whined. "Just tell me."

"Patience is a virtue." He couldn't help himself. She was just so much fun to tease.

"I've been patient for almost a year now," Molly muttered, probably to herself. But Jake heard, and the thought froze him halfway through preparing his next snowball.

"Yeah?"

She rolled her eyes. "What do you think? I haven't seen you since last New Year."

"Yes, but…" Did she mean she'd been thinking about him all year, the way he'd been thinking about her? Or did she mean she hadn't been with anyone else since? Or even both?

She fixed him with a level gaze. "You're not that easy to get out of the system, it turns out."

"Neither are you," he admitted. It wasn't quite a full confession – she didn't need to know how many work hours had been lost to daydreaming about what might have happened if Tim hadn't walked in when he had. Especially since most of them had been followed up by mental chastisement, knowing that it was for the best that they'd been interrupted, or they might have done something they'd both regret.

But things were different now. One way or another, if he got Molly alone again, Jake was certain he'd never regret it.

And he'd make sure she didn't either.

# Chapter 14

By the time they'd called a ceasefire, finished Tim's snowman, and all retreated back inside, it was almost time for Christmas lunch – and Molly was still thinking about Jake. In fact, it seemed like that might be a permanent situation – at least until she found a way to get him out of her system.

She had a list of great ideas for that, just as soon as the opportunity presented itself.

Molly changed out of her soggy jeans and sweater and, in a fit of festive optimism, slipped into some of the lacy lingerie she'd packed. Just in case.

Of course, she couldn't be too obvious. So she pulled out the deep red knitted dress her parents had bought her for Christmas and tugged it over her head, pairing it with some thick black tights. Perfectly Christmassy and respectable. No one would guess a thing.

Except, hopefully, Jake.

And with that thought, she skipped down for lunch.

Three courses later, Molly was stuffed. As her dad loaded the dishwasher, she made a mental promise to clear up every day between Boxing Day and New Year, just as long as she didn't have to move from the table for at least an hour.

"Well. I think this has been a highly successful Christmas."

Philippa leant back in her chair, surveying the remains of the Christmas pudding. "Fifteen sorts of mince pie, some lovely presents, and a lovely lunch."

"And it's not over yet," Dory pointed out. "We've still got the Doctor Who Christmas Special to watch."

"Actually, before that, I've got one more present to give you." Lucas got to his feet and held out a hand to Dory. Molly looked for Jake, but he'd disappeared.

This must be what he'd meant when he said she'd find out after dinner.

They all followed Lucas and Dory back through to the lounge, curiosity outweighing the need to digest. Molly stopped at the doorway and smiled. Jake stood by the tree, holding Tim's iPod speakers. As he pressed play, the sound of Wham!'s *Last Christmas* started playing.

Dory raised her eyebrows at Lucas. "Is this supposed to be a musical clue?"

Smiling, Lucas dropped down to one knee, and Molly gasped. "This might be a better clue."

Eyes wide and one hand at her mouth, Dory nodded.

"I have no idea why you like this song," Lucas started, and Dory laughed. "It's not romantic, and George Michael has really weird hair in the video. But you love it, and the thing is… last Christmas, you changed my life. You took all the things that were screwing me up and you, I don't know. Made them not matter any more, I guess. You showed me what I really wanted – needed, even. And it turns out, what I need most in my life, is you."

Molly caught Jake's eye, and knew he was thinking the same thing she was – that their own last Christmas story didn't have quite so romantic an ending.

Maybe she could change that tonight.

"I wanted to ask you this question here, with your family, on your favourite day of the year," Lucas went on. "Partly because I figured you might have had enough wine at lunch to actually say yes, but mostly because… this is who you are. This family made you the woman I love more than anything."

Behind her, Molly heard her mum sniff. Mum loved Lucas. She loved Jake too, of course, but in a different way. Molly looked down at the bracelet on her wrist. What would Mum say if she and Jake suddenly stopped sneaking around and kissed in front of everyone?

Actually, never mind Mum. What the hell would *Dad* do?

"Dorothea Mackenzie. Will you do me the incredible honour of being my wife?"

"Of course I will!" Dory dragged Lucas up to his feet and kissed him, as the rest of them applauded. Leaving the music playing, Jake found his way across to Molly, and she grinned up at him.

"This is what Lucas was talking to you about earlier?"

He nodded. "And, I think we can all agree; this Christmas is officially memorable."

"That it is." Molly ran her fingers across her snowflake charm. "And like Tim said, it's not over yet."

She caught Jake's gaze with her own and swallowed at the heat she saw there. Tonight, one way or another, they were going to settle things between them. She couldn't take the anticipation any longer. She needed to know.

"Oh!" Dory yelped, and Molly tore her eyes away. "It's time for Doctor Who!"

"I still don't understand what happened with the aliens," her mum said, as the credits rolled. Dory started to explain, but Tim interrupted.

"Never mind them. I've got a much more important question. Why do we have to have sprouts every year when no one actually likes them." Tim was still wearing his cracker hat, although it had slipped over one ear at some point when the Doctor had been saving someone, and his wine glass was empty again.

90

"It's traditional," her mum said. "It wouldn't be Christmas without them. Just like it wouldn't be Christmas without my family around me."

Molly smiled at the sentiment but, when she glanced up, she caught her dad and Jake exchanging a loaded glance. Tim was staring at his hands, and Dory had her lower lip between her teeth as she looked at Lucas.

Suddenly, it struck Molly. This was the last Christmas it would be this way, all of them together. Dory and Lucas were going to want to spend at least some years in America – especially once they were married. Tim would be leaving for Switzerland in a few days and who knew if he'd be able to get home every Christmas. And she... well, she'd still be coming home. At this rate, it would be her and Jake at the dinner table every year.

Which didn't sound as awful a prospect as it would have done, a year ago.

"Well, I think Lucas and I are going to bed." The smile on Dory's face would have been totally inappropriate for family time, if she hadn't just got engaged.

As everyone wished them goodnight, Molly caught Jake's eye again. *Two down...*

Mum was next, pleading tiredness after all the cooking. She reminded them all about the leftovers that needed eating, then disappeared upstairs. *Two to go...*

Molly felt a tightness growing in her belly with every passing moment, and her brain had taken to chanting, *soon, soon, soon,* over the soundtrack of whichever James Bond movie they were watching.

Tim fell asleep on the sofa half way through the film. It took Dad a moment or two to notice, but once he did he prodded him in the side. "You awake there, Tim?"

"Wha...?" Tim's eyes opened briefly, then closed again.

Dad looked up at Jake. "Think he's ready for bed, too. Help me get him up there? I don't fancy trying to pour him up those attic stairs."

"Of course." Jake hoisted Tim up and slung his arm over his shoulder.

"Want me to pause the film?" Molly asked, because she couldn't exactly say, 'are you coming back?' in front of her dad.

"That would be great." Jake's smile told her he knew exactly what she was doing. Still, she didn't see him objecting.

"Think I'll head up too," Dad said, stretching. "Don't you two stay up too late now, will you?"

"Yes, Dad." The knot grew tighter in Molly's middle as she watched them process out of the room. Once they were out of sight, she stared at the frozen image on the television, counting down the seconds until Jake came back.

She hadn't thought this through at all. What the hell was she going to say? Or do? Beyond putting on some fancy knickers, she'd barely considered what happened next.

Well. That wasn't entirely true. Back in London, late at night, she'd imagined the scene a thousand different ways. She'd just never bothered thinking about the conversation they needed to have *before* they got to the good stuff.

Footsteps on the stairs and then, too soon, Jake was back. He stood, watching her from the doorway and Molly bit her lip under his scrutiny. One of them was going to have to say something, to start the conversation…

Slowly, deliberately, as if giving her time to object, Jake closed the lounge door, and they were completely alone.

"Jake, I know we need to—"

"Shhh." Stepping closer, he bent down and put a finger to her lips. "Let's talk… later."

Mutely, Molly nodded. He was right. How could they talk when every feeling they'd been trying to suppress for the last year was coursing through them, trying to break free?

And when Jake pressed a kiss to her lips, it definitely felt like freedom.

Oh God, this woman would be the death of him. How could one kiss, one simple, soft kiss, render him so incapable of thought? His only priority when she was near was keeping her there; his only wish to be allowed to touch and kiss her some more.

And for the first time ever, there was no one there who would want to stop him. Especially not Molly.

Her hands reached up around his waist to press against his back, pulling him down towards her. Without breaking the kiss, Jake got to his knees, kneeling between her thighs as she sat on the sofa, bringing himself down to the same level.

"Hi," Molly said, pulling away just far enough to look into his eyes. "I missed you."

"I've been right here." His words came out hoarse, and he knew she had to be able to hear his desperation. His need.

She shook her head, just enough for her hair to tickle his cheek. "Not here, here you haven't." She pulled him closer and kissed him again. "I missed you right here."

"I'll make it up to you," he promised.

Molly's smile turned wicked. "Oh good. I so hoped you would."

Jake felt a moment's loss for the thought of his king-sized bed at home looking out over green fields, and the pleasures he could give her if they were there and truly alone. But it had already been so long, he knew neither of them were willing to wait.

He stripped off her dress and laid her out on the sofa before him, all lace and loveliness, her flushed skin glowing in the firelight. "God, you're beautiful."

"And you're still clothed," Molly pointed out, wriggling her tights down over her hips, revealing the matching knickers he'd last seen strewn across the driveway.

"Sorry." Jake yanked his jumper over his head, ignoring the part of his brain that reminded him that there were still other people in the house. People who could walk in and find him debauching the baby of the family any minute now.

But God, that debauching would be worth it. Worth everything that might happen next.

"Do you have…" Molly trailed off, her lower lip caught between her teeth.

"Of course." Jake pulled the condom from the back pocket of his jeans and placed it on the arm of the sofa. "But we don't need it just yet."

At her frustrated look, he flashed her a smile and lowered his mouth to her breasts. After all, just because they didn't have the luxury of privacy, a bed, or anything else, didn't mean he couldn't make this a night she'd never forget.

And hopefully one she'd want to repeat.

# Chapter 15

**BOXING DAY**

Molly had lost all track of time – and her underwear – but it had to be after midnight. Lying naked on her parents' sofa, her head resting against Jake's bare chest, covered only by the fleecy blanket her mum kept thrown over the back of the sofa for cold nights, wasn't exactly how she'd intended to spend Christmas Day evening.

But God, she didn't regret one moment of it.

"We need to do that again, in a bed," she said, almost without thinking.

Jake hummed his agreement, already half asleep as far as she could tell.

Did he snore? Molly had no idea. He'd been in her life since before she was born, but there was still so much she didn't know about him. Was she going to get the chance to learn?

And did she want it?

She wanted to sleep with him again, that was a definite. The man had given her the best sex of her life on a sofa with her parents upstairs – not really the ideal sort of conditions for these things. Imagine what more he could do if he had her alone, in a bed, for as long as they wanted…

If he wanted it. What if it hadn't been so fantastic for him? No, that was stupid. She'd seen his face the moment before he finished inside her. It had been *awesome* for him too. *She* had been awesome.

But fantastic sex and ridiculous chemistry weren't everything. He might have this every day of the week with his string of elegant brunettes. And even if he didn't… she still wasn't confident he wanted *her* for the right reasons.

Of course, he hadn't actually told her he wanted her for more than one night…

God, couldn't she just lie back and enjoy the afterglow? Tomorrow, she could deconstruct the whole thing with Lara, or call Jenna and tell she had risen to the challenge. Or rather, Jake had.

She bit back a laugh. This was ridiculous. She was supposed to be a grown woman now, but here she was having sex on her parents' sofa because she didn't have anywhere else to go, and thinking about what she'd tell her friends tomorrow. She might as well be sixteen and back in school again.

No, the only person she needed to discuss this with was lying beneath her on this couch.

Sighing, Jake shifted to raise himself up on his elbow, looking down at her. "What are you obsessing about? I can practically hear your thoughts whirring."

"Just thinking about how this feels like me circa age sixteen," Molly admitting, waving a hand to indicate the sofa.

Jake raised an eyebrow. "Not all of it, I hope."

"No, not all of it." Her cheeks felt warm at the memory of him inside her. She'd definitely never had anyone like Jake when she was sixteen.

"Which parts, then?" Jake asked.

"Location, mostly," Molly admitted. "Almost had me thinking about what I was going to tell my friends at school tomorrow."

"Oh God, you're going to tell Lara, and she's going to tease me about it for all time."

"Probably," Molly admitted. "But actually, I was mostly thinking about my friend Jenna, in London. I promised I'd let her know if…" she trailed off, realising too late what she was about to admit.

"Let her know if you managed to get me into bed?" Jake guessed.

Molly's cheeks burned as she nodded.

"So, you had a plan for this?" Jake shook his head. "I should have known. Especially after your suitcase burst open."

"I wasn't exactly subtle about it," Molly pointed out. "Besides, Jenna challenged me. You were my last unfilled resolution."

"Resolution?" Jake's forehead crinkled up in confusion. It was a cute look on him.

"Yeah." Molly snuggled a little closer for warmth, and covered her mouth as she yawned. "This year is the first time ever I've managed to actually keep all my new year's resolutions."

"And I was one of them?" Jake asked, his voice curiously flat. "What were the others?"

Molly ticked them off on her fingers. "Move to London, get a real job, and sleep with you."

"And you scored the full hat-trick."

"I did." She smiled up at him. "But I definitely think this one was my favourite."

She'd expected him to kiss her, or to return the smile at least. But instead, Jake stared down at her, his eyes cool and assessing.

"And, I mean, that wasn't the only reason I… that we…"

"Had sex," Jake finished for her. "I should hope we're both grown up enough to actually say it."

"Of course. It's just… the other two things had been on my list for years, and after last New Year's Eve, I added the one about you almost as a joke. Except not, because I really, really wanted it. I just didn't think that you did."

"Why? Because I stopped kissing you when your brother walked in? That was just self-preservation, Molly."

"Because you avoided me afterwards. You didn't even come to my leaving party."

"Did you ever think I just didn't want to see you go?"

Molly stilled at his words. She'd been cross with him for six months about not showing up for that party, and with twelve words he'd cut away all that anger.

"Is that true?"

Jake sucked in a deep breath, and lay back down beside her, pulling her head onto his chest before he spoke again. "I wanted you to go because it was what you wanted. You've talked for years about moving to London and getting a job that didn't involve working weekends and holidays."

"Turns out you might be the only one who took that talk seriously," Molly muttered, but he didn't react to it.

"I wanted you to have the life you dreamt of. Still do. But the selfish part of me? That part really didn't want to see you move two hundred miles away."

"Why not?" Molly was almost afraid of the answer, but she couldn't not ask.

"Why do you think?" Jake sat up, the blanket falling away from his perfect chest. "Molly—"

He cut off as the lounge door opened, and they both twisted to see who it was.

"Are you two – Oh God! Sorry… I… Never mind." Dory shut the door firmly behind her, as Molly felt the panic rising in her chest. This truly was her teenage years all over again. Humiliation, and the possibility of ruining everything through sheer stupidity.

"I need to talk to her. I need… clothes, to start with." She could reason with Dory. Her sister had kept her secrets before. No one needed to know how badly she'd screwed this up – risking one of the most important friendships in not just her life, but her whole family, just to keep some stupid resolution. To win a dare with a friend she'd only known six months. What had she been thinking?

Jake handed her dress over. "What are you going to say to her?"

"What do you think?" Molly tugged the dress over her head. Underwear and tights would have to wait. "I'm going to tell her it was a mulled wine fuelled mistake and beg her never to tell my parents. Or Tim." That, at least, should make Jake happy. "As long as no one else ever finds out, it can be like this never happened. We can go back to how we were before."

"Do you really believe that?" Jake was still naked, sprawled on the couch before her, the blanket barely covering all the relevant parts.

"Why aren't you panicking about this more?"

"Because what's done is done. We just need to figure out what we want to do next."

"No." Nothing was ever that simple. And if she screwed this up, she knew her family would never let her forget it. It would be one more flaky Molly story to tell at Christmas dinners long to come. "What we need to do is make it look like it never happened at all."

And with that, she left the man she'd been fantasising about all year naked on the sofa and went to talk to her sister.

The kitchen light was on and, when Molly walked in, she found Dory making tea in the tiny stainless steel pot only she ever used.

"Okay, so what you saw…" Molly started, but Dory cut her off.

"I *told* Tim I wasn't imagining that there was something different between you and Jake this year."

"I know. I heard. You told him that if he told me not to get involved with Jake it would be the first thing I'd go out and do."

Dory winced. "You weren't meant to hear that. But, you know, I was kind of right."

"No you weren't." Molly shut the door behind her and sank into the nearest kitchen chair. "It's not… it wasn't like that."

Grabbing two cups and saucers from the shelf, Dory poured them both tea. "Then tell me what it was like," she said, placing one cup in front of Molly.

Molly scrunched up her nose at the smell. "Peppermint?"

"It's calming," Dory said, sitting opposite her. "And, after three courses plus mince pies, good for the digestion. Now, talk."

Where to start? "Well, you remember last New Year's Eve?"

It took embarrassingly little time to recap everything that had happened between her and Jake in the last year, mostly because hardly anything had. Until tonight.

"So what now?" Dory asked. "Was this really just a one night thing to fulfil some stupid resolution?"

"I thought it was." Molly swallowed, remembering Jake lying there telling her what was done was done. "I thought that was all *he* would want either. But now… I don't understand why he'd suddenly be willing to risk everything." Although she had a horrible feeling it had more to do with her family than her.

"Don't you?" Dory gave her a small smile. "Then maybe you should ask him."

# Chapter 16

The front doorstep was cold through his jeans, and Jake wished he'd taken time to grab his coat when he got dressed. But he'd needed fresh air, needed to move away from that room, to get out of the house, even if he hadn't gone far. The front door was on the latch behind him, and he could vaguely make out Dory and Molly's voices in the kitchen, although not what they were saying.

He could imagine, though. Molly was probably explaining to her sister how this whole thing was a big mistake. A stupid resolution she had to follow through on. One night only.

As if he could go back to being her pseudo-big brother now. Back to pretending there was nothing between them. He'd had a taste of her now, a preview of everything they could be together.

Except she was heading back to London on the second of January, and hadn't so much as hinted that their relationship might last beyond tonight. Instead, she'd pretty much confirmed the opposite.

He'd thought it wouldn't matter and that if this was his last Mackenzie Christmas, at least it could be the best yet. One he'd remember his whole life.

Well, he'd managed that much. No way was he forgetting this one in a hurry.

But he'd thought he'd be able to move on, live his life without looking back. And that, he knew now, was impossible.

That damn fortune telling fish was right. He was in love with Molly Mackenzie, and he hadn't even realised it until the moment she said that sleeping with him was a mistake.

God, how much more could he have screwed this one up?

"Jake?" The door creaked open behind him and Molly stood there, fully clothed now in tights and, presumably, underwear. "What are you doing out here?" She stepped out and sat down beside him, wincing at the cold stone.

"Thinking."

"About?"

"What happens next."

Wrapping her arms around her knees, Molly looked up at him, her eyes wide and green even in the faint light from the hall. "And what have you decided?"

Wasn't that the ultimate question? Except, it wasn't entirely up to him, was it?

But some of it could be. He could take charge of his own life, even if he had no say in hers. He could stop waiting to be kicked out, to finally outstay his welcome. Instead of always waiting for the other shoe to drop, he could move on, like everyone else had.

"I think it's time for me to go home." The words felt good, right. Just making a decision felt like a step forward.

"You're supposed to be staying until New Year," Molly said, her voice even. "Mum will be sad if you miss the party."

"I'll come back for the party." One last hurrah before he made his own resolutions for the next year.

"And we still haven't really talked. About us." Was that fear in her eyes? Or just confusion? Jake couldn't tell.

"I think we've said all we need to, don't you? You got what you wanted – your one night to complete your list of resolutions. And you said all along that that should be enough to get it out of our systems, right?" He just hadn't believed her. Had known that if he gave in to that temptation, one night would never be enough – and he'd fooled himself into thinking it would be the same for her.

"Dory's not going to say anything," Molly said, the words coming out a little rushed. "I mean, you don't need to worry about Tim, or Dad, or anything. No one will know. It can just be like it was before. Right?"

Did she honestly believe that? Or was she just trying to make herself feel better? Jake couldn't tell. But if she *was* feeling bad about everything, then she had to know that his expectations were rather different from hers.

After days of not managing a full conversation, it was finally time to put everything on the table.

"Look, Molly. This is the situation as I see it." Laying out the blueprints for what might have been, he wanted to show her that what they'd actually created missed the mark. "After last year, I knew that I wanted you. That I was attracted to you. But I also knew I couldn't do anything about it. If you didn't feel the same – or even if you did, but things didn't last – I'd be risking not just upsetting your whole family, but losing my place here. Your family matter to me, Molly."

"I know that." She pulled a face, then looked down at her knees, twisting the fabric of her dress between her fingers. "That's why I couldn't figure out what had changed. Why you were suddenly willing to risk it."

Jake sighed. It had all seemed so logical at the time. Now he felt like he'd twisted every fact and possibility to fit what he wanted – Molly Mackenzie naked.

"I figured that this was the last Christmas we were all likely to be together like this. With Tim moving overseas, Dory and Lucas getting married… things are changing. And there won't be a place here for me any more."

Her body tensed beside him. "And so you thought that if you seduced me, maybe even pretended to love me, you'd always have a place in my family, right?"

"What? No!"

"It's okay, Jake." She huffed a small, sad laugh. "I always knew they mattered to you more than I did."

"You've got this all wrong, Molly." Panic was rising in his chest now, more potent than mulled wine and heavier than mince pies. "And anyway, how the hell can you say I seduced you?" That wasn't the point. He needed to focus. "Look, I didn't even realise it, even after the thing with the fish—"

"The fish?" Molly stared at him in confusion. "Jake, seriously, stop. It's okay. I'm going back to London soon anyway. Like you said, I got what I wanted from this. And Dory won't talk, so you get what you need too. We don't have to be together, or anything. I'll still be coming home every Christmas, so of course there's a place for you here. You're family."

"No." The word came out stronger and louder than Jake had intended, and Molly flinched away from him. But he had to say this. He had to make her understand. "I'm not family. I'm *definitely* not your brother. And I won't come back here every year and watch you getting on with your life without me, Molly. I can't sit back and see you find some guy down there and bringing him home to meet the family. I thought I could. I thought I could let you go live your life and just watch from the sidelines. But I can't because I'm in love with you."

*Don't gape, Molly. It's rude.*

Okay, she really didn't need her mother's voice in her head at a time like this. She didn't know *what* she needed, but it wasn't etiquette advice.

"No you're not." She winced as soon as the words were out. Challenging someone else's feelings wasn't terribly polite either. But, really, he *wasn't*. He couldn't be.

Could he?

"Trust me, Molly, my life would be a hell of a lot easier if it wasn't true." Jake sighed, sounding bone weary. "Look, it's okay. I'll get over it. You have your dream life now. I know that, and I'm not going to stand in your way of getting back to it."

Her dream life. London. Molly wasn't sure whether to laugh at herself or cry when she remembered the original plan. Sleep with Jake and get it out of her system, so that she could go forth and seduce the handsome young men of London next year.

As if any of them held a candle to Jake.

But love? That was something different altogether. That was the kind of thing you really didn't want to screw up, or flake out on. Especially when it meant risking hurting one of the most important people in your life.

And Jake had always been that, long before last New Year's Eve.

"I don't know what to say. Or do. Or…" She took a deep breath. "What do you want from me?"

"From you? Nothing at all."

"But I…" What? Want to make it better? Like a child's bumped knee or a middle school fallout that could be resolved with a muttered *sorry* and a new game?

Jake inhaled, low and calmly, then got to his feet. "I'm going to go home for a few days, like I said. I'll be back on New Year's Eve and, after that, you won't have to see me again if you don't want to."

"Of course I want to! I just…"

"Yeah. Exactly." Bending down, he kissed her on the top of the head. "Get some sleep. I'll see you on the thirty first."

He headed inside, and Molly listened to his footsteps all the way up the stairs, until they faded as he got towards the attic. But she sat there in the cold until she couldn't feel anything any more.

# Chapter 17

**NEW YEAR'S EVE**

"I can't believe you have to work New Year's Eve." Molly straightened the registration forms for loyalty cards on the hotel's front desk. "You'll miss the party."

"You mean I won't be there to protect you from Jake," Lara said, rolling her eyes. "Besides, you've worked more New Year's than I have in the last five years. In fact, if you'd been working *last* year you wouldn't even be in this mess."

"Very helpful. Thank you."

"Be honest, you miss it." Lara leant across the reception desk. "Don't you?"

Molly considered. "More than I thought I would," she admitted. "It's not that I don't like my new job. It's just that, well, every day is kind of the same."

"Sounds boring," Lara said. "Unlike your love life. So, come on. Have you decided what you're going to tell your poor lovelorn Jake?"

"He's not lovelorn. Or mine. Or anything, really. If he shows up at the party tonight he'll probably just blame it all on the mulled wine and go back to ignoring me for the next year. Nothing to worry about."

Lara gave Molly a long look, one that seemed to see too deeply inside her. "Is that what you're hoping for, or what you're afraid of?"

Damn it. Lara really had known her too long and too well. "Both."

"Thought so." Lara sighed. "Sorry I can't be there with you."

Molly shrugged. "I'm a big girl now. I can handle it."

"Yeah. Big city girl and everything. Like Liverpool isn't city enough for anyone." There was more bite to Lara's voice than Molly expected. She shot her friend an inquisitive look. "Sorry. Just miss you, I guess."

"I miss you too." Molly gave her an apologetic smile. "Part of me wishes I'd stayed here instead of moving to London."

"Then move back," Lara said, as if it were as easy as changing outfits.

"Yes, please, for the love of God, do." Krissie, Molly's old boss, appeared behind the desk looking rather frazzled. "I need a day off with someone I can trust in charge."

"My replacement not up to scratch?" Molly allowed herself a small smile. Nice to know she wasn't easily replaceable.

"The three replacements we've been through in the last six months, you mean," Krissie replied. "And no. Not a patch on you."

Molly winced. "Sorry."

"That's okay." Krissie sighed. "I know you had to go and follow your dream or whatever. I just wish your dream had been to take over the events department here or something."

Huh. The events department. She'd helped out there often enough when they were short handed, and loved the racing around and the way no two days were ever the same. Why hadn't it occurred to her to ask about working there full time?

"I never even thought of that," she admitted.

"Of course, personally, I was hoping you'd want my job when I inevitably get promoted to being in charge of everything," Krissie said, leaning her elbows on the reception desk and resting her chin in her hands. "But events would have worked too. Ah well.

Too late now."

Yes, it was. Because she had her new life in London, and her respectable job that gave her weekends and holidays off, and she couldn't take the humiliation of another backwards step. Of admitting, once again, that she had no idea where she was going or what she was doing in life.

But even knowing that didn't stop her asking. "So, hypothetically, if I ever needed to move back to Liverpool in a hurry… there might be a job for me here?"

"No *might* about it, love. I'd have you back in an instant." Krissie patted her arm as she headed off back to work. "Think about it, yeah? You're wasted stuck at some computer all day."

"Yeah, but at least she doesn't have to work New Year's Eve," Lara called after her, and Molly laughed. She really had missed this place.

Almost as much as she missed Jake.

By six o'clock on New Year's Eve, the office was deserted, except for Jake. He'd figured there was no point rushing his arrival at the Mackenzies' party, so he might as well get some more work done first. Especially since it looked like work was *all* he was going to be doing for the foreseeable future.

The receptionist had knocked off at four, and most of the secretaries had taken the day as holiday anyway, so when the lift opened onto his floor Jake knew there was no one out there to greet their visitor. And nobody but him there for them to see.

He had a whole 'sorry, the office is closed, come back next year,' speech ready, but when he stepped out into the reception area and saw Glen Mackenzie waiting for him, he realised it was going to be useless. When the man who had taken you in and treated you like a son came visiting, opening hours, schedules and personal preferences went by the wayside.

Especially when you'd seduced the man's daughter on his own sofa less than a week ago.

"Glen. Philippa send you to check I'm still coming to the party?" It seemed like the most likely scenario. Molly's mother hadn't been exactly happy when she'd caught him skipping out in the early hours of Boxing Day – especially since he hadn't had much of an explanation to help her understand why.

"She doesn't know I'm here, actually." Glen's expression was more serious than Jake had seen it since he and Tim were underage teenagers in trouble for sneaking off to some nightclub. "Can we sit? Might make this easier."

"Of course." That didn't bode well either. Jake ushered him over to the comfortable waiting area of the reception, and let him settle on a bright yellow armchair before he took a seat on the sofa opposite.

"So, um," Jake started, then trailed off. What was he supposed to say to this man?

"Jake, I think this is going to be less awful for both of us if you just let me talk for a bit. Then afterwards, I'll go home, and when I see you at the party later we can pretend this never happens. If you still want to come to the party, of course."

Oh, he really, really didn't like the sound of this. "Okay."

"Where to start?" Glen stared at a point somewhere over Jake's left shoulder. Somehow he got the impression that this wasn't going to be any easier for Glen than for him. "When you've been married a long time, you learn all the little things about each other. You learn to put up with each other's little quirks and oddities. Like the way Philippa always has to sleep with earplugs in, no matter where we are and how quiet it is. She blames my snoring, but I think she just likes the fact that nothing can wake her up until she's ready."

He smiled at Jake like it was a shared joke, but Jake really wasn't seeing anything funny about this day yet. "Right."

"And Phil, well she's learned to put up with the fact that I always have to sleep with the window a little bit open. Always. Even in the dead of winter. Even on Christmas Day."

Christmas Day. The words froze in the air between them and every muscle in Jake's body tensed. Philippa and Glen's bedroom was at the front of the house. Glen's open window would be right over the front door… right over the step where Jake and Molly had argued that night.

Oh God. If Glen had heard everything, he could probably guess exactly what Jake had done to Molly on that sofa. And, quite honestly, Jake was surprised to still be alive.

"Sir." Since when had he ever called Glen sir? "I can explain. Well, no, I can't. I can only apologise—"

"Jake. Let me finish talking." Glen's voice was unnaturally calm. It made Jake nervous.

"Okay."

"My children are grown adults now. They get to choose what they want to do with their lives, whether I approve of it or not. I didn't want Dory to move to New York with that rat of an ex-fiancé of hers, but it worked out for the best. She'd never have met Lucas if she hadn't, and she's happy now." For one brief second, a misty smile floated across Glen's face before he added, "And I have a wedding to pay for. But that's beside the point. I don't know if moving to Switzerland is going to make Tim happy, but I have to let him try. I didn't want Molly to move to London, and if I could tell her to stop being so stubborn and making herself miserable and just come home, I would. But I can't, because she's an adult now. Even if maybe we don't always treat her that way."

Jake looked down at his hands. He was as guilty of that as anyone. Molly had been the baby for so long, it was hard sometimes to remember that she'd ever grown up. To take her decisions seriously. He hadn't, when this whole mess had started. He'd assumed he needed to be the adult, to put the brakes on things. By the time he'd realised she was old enough to make her own choices, he'd already made them all for her.

Which is why he was standing back this time. Whatever happened next, it had to be up to her.

"The point is, whatever is going on between the two of you is exactly that – between the two of you. And while I might desperately wish you'd chosen to have that discussion somewhere other than under my window, I can't unhear it now. And it did make one thing clear to me – something I should have said to you a long time ago and haven't."

Glen wasn't staring over his left shoulder anymore. Instead, Molly's father was looking him straight in the eyes and Jake realised he was holding his breath, waiting for a sentence.

"Jake. You've been like a son to me since you were about ten, and I realise you've spent more time in our home than in your own. Whatever happens in your life, you will always be a son to me. And you will always, always be welcome in my house, at Christmas or any other time of the year. You might not need the same kind of support as my other children have over the years – I can't see you choosing to move in for a start. But if you ever needed to, you could. So don't run away from us, because we'll never turn our backs on you."

How much had Jake needed to hear that? And how had he not known that was what he needed until this moment?

But Glen wasn't done. "You lost your own parents too young, and it was tragic. I would never presume to take their place. But in my heart, you are my son, and I realised I'd never told you that."

Jake couldn't move. Couldn't respond, couldn't think, couldn't do anything except let the words soak in until they felt true. He knew he should say something, acknowledge the moment and the huge gift he'd just been given.

But instead he sat and stared and let the moment happen. And it felt wonderful.

Glen pushed against the arm of the chair and got slowly to his feet. "Been a long holiday this one. And, I should mention, because Philippa will kill me if I don't – Molly's been miserable without you. Even if she won't admit it. " Jake's gaze flew up to Glen's face and found an amused smile there.

"And by the way," Glen added, already halfway to the lifts. "I have a feeling you'd make an even better son-in-law."

# Chapter 18

"Are you guys ready?" Tim stuck his head through the door, and Molly waved her mascara wand at him.

"Does it look like we're ready?" Beside her, Dory was jostling for space in front of the mirror, and it was giving Molly flashbacks to her early teen years. Why couldn't she get ready in her own room, anyway? "Besides, the party doesn't start for ages, and everything's ready downstairs. What's the rush?"

"Not ready for the party," Tim said, pushing through the door and dropping down to lounge on the spare twin bed. "For this." He held up a spiral pad and a pen.

"I'm ready." Dory bounced onto the bed beside him, her make up inexplicably finished and perfect.

"What, exactly, is *this*?" Molly asked suspiciously.

"It's time to make our new year's resolutions," Dory said with a grin. "Come on."

Just the thought of it made Molly's heart clench, and her mind fill with Jake again. Not that *that* was much of a surprise. Almost everything did.

"I don't think I'm going to make any this year." After all, look how badly last year's had turned out.

"Of course you are. Sit down, Moll." Tim pointed at the opposite bed and, screwing her mascara wand back into the tube, Molly did as she was told.

How much did Tim know? He'd been strangely… nice to her, since Jake left. Molly had a strong suspicion that Dory might have got to him.

"Okay, I'll start," Dory said, taking the pen and notebook from Tim. "This year, I resolve not to become an utter bridezilla, but to plan a brilliant wedding that Lucas and I will remember for the rest of our lives."

Molly pulled a face. Making resolutions was easy when you had your life all sorted, obviously.

"I'll believe it when I see it," Tim said. "The bridezilla bit, I mean. I'm sure you'll have the rest perfectly in hand as always. Now give that here."

Resting the notebook on his bent knee, he sucked on the end of the pen as he thought. "I resolve to… what do I resolve to do, Dory?"

Dory rolled her eyes. "I don't know! Um, make the most of your new life in Switzerland and find a girlfriend?"

"Works for me." Tim shrugged and wrote it down. "And I resolve to have a dry January. Let my liver recover from all this mulled wine." He tossed the pad and pen at Molly. "Your turn."

"I told you. I'm not making any. I'm taking my clean sweep of resolutions from this year and declaring myself done with them."

"Clean sweep?" Tim asked. "What were your resolutions last year?"

Molly squirmed. "You know. Get a nine to five job. Move to London."

"Sleep with Jake," Dory added.

"Dory!" It came out as a squeal. How could she? Just what she *didn't* want Tim to know.

Except… Tim was laughing. "Why are you laughing?"

"Because I can't believe you made sleeping with my best friend an honest to God resolution," Tim said, between sniggers. "Couldn't you just get him drunk and drag him to bed like a normal person?"

"I thought... you said..." Molly gave up trying to find the words. He knew what she meant.

"Well, I'm not saying I'm over the moon about it," Tim said, sobering up. "But Dory tells me it's not just another one-night stand, at least on his part. She might also have mentioned something about you being a grown up now, but I'm not sure I believe that."

"You should," Molly said, absently. Tim had a point. Making sleeping with Jake a resolution? That was childish. Well, adolescent, at least. Figuring out where they went from here; that would be the grown up thing to do.

Even if she just wanted to run away to London and try to pretend nothing ever happened.

"To be honest, I'm more worried about you breaking his delicate little heart," Tim said. "I mean, you've already ruined my plans for spending my last week in Britain in the pub with my best mate. So what I want to know is, what are you going to do about it?"

"I got us into this mess," Molly said. "So I'll get us out." Jake might have ignored her texts last year, and avoided her – which was not the most grown up behaviour either. But she was the one who'd pushed and pushed to get what she wanted, without thinking beyond New Year's Eve. And here she was, on the brink of a new year, and she still didn't have a plan for what was going to have next.

Perhaps it was time to make one.

Molly picked up the pen. "I resolve to make decisions based on what's best for me, my future, and the people I love. Not what I *think* other people want, or what other people tell me I'm *supposed* to want."

"To thine ownself be true," Dory quoted softly. "Sounds like a plan."

Molly nodded, and wrote it down. "And I'm starting this resolution a few hours early."

Jake could hear the music long before he knocked on the front door of the Mackenzie's house. The Waitresses were blaring out of the Tim's iPod speakers, which he assumed meant that Molly had taken control of the playlist. She had an unholy love for that song.

He took a breath to steel himself for the thought of Molly. Of his last conversation with her on this step. He'd been haunted by her memory for the last five days, and now he had to face her again. He'd done everything he could – given her time and space to think about them and the things he'd said.

Now he had to find out her decision. And he really wasn't sure he wanted to know.

Glen said she'd been miserable without him, but was that just guilt? And even if she decided she wanted to try a relationship between them, he was under no illusions about the difficulty of maintaining a long distance relationship.

The door opened, revealing Philippa in her best red sequinned frock. "You came! Oh Jake, I'm so pleased. Come in, come in. Everyone is in the front room – Dory and Lucas are opening engagement cards and presents."

"Right. I brought them something…" He started to hold up the bottle of Prosecco with ribbon around it, but then he spotted Molly standing at the foot of the stairs, her auburn hair loose around her beautiful face.

"I'll put it to chill," Philippa said, taking the bottle and disappearing into the kitchen.

"I thought you weren't coming," Molly said after a long moment in which they just stared at each other stupidly.

"I said I'd be here," Jake reminded her. "Besides, I had a visit from your dad. Made it clear I was expected."

Molly winced. "Warning you away from his little girl?"

"No." Quite the opposite, in fact. Jake stepped closer, wanting to touch her but knowing he couldn't, not just yet. Not until he knew her decision. "He told me you were an adult, capable of making your own choices."

"Oh." Her eyes widened in surprise. "Dory told Tim the same thing."

"Tim knows?" Because Glen being okay with it was one thing. Tim was a whole other issue.

"He laughed. A lot." She gave a little half shrug. "I think he's decided I'm not good enough for you now, instead."

"Never happen. He's your big brother. No one will ever be good enough for you."

"What else did Dad say?" Molly leaned back against the bottom of the banister, her arms folded across her middle. It made the drapey tunic dress thing she was wearing ride up a little, and Jake had to focus on not staring at her legs.

She really did have incredible legs.

"Uh, a few things," Jake said, trying to get his mind back on track. "That I'd always have a place here, for one. Whatever happens." Maybe later, or one day, he'd share the whole conversation with her. But tonight, they had more important things to talk about.

"That's… that's good." Molly took a breath, held it, then blew it out again without speaking.

"You've made a decision," Jake guessed. "One you don't think I'm going to like."

Molly looked up at him, her pale green eyes looking wider than ever fringed with thick black lashes. "I didn't make a decision. I made a new resolution."

Oh good. Because that wasn't what had got them into this mess in the first place, or anything.

But it was her turn to be the grown up. His turn to listen. So he said, "Tell me."

Molly's heart was beating too quickly as she stepped closer, as though she had a phone on vibrate inside her ribcage. She wanted to touch him, to feel his solidity under her hands, just to prove to herself that he really had come back. He'd given her a chance to make things right between them.

Now she just had to not screw it up.

"It's like you said. I'm an adult now. Not because I moved to London, or got a job some place new. But because I'm finally ready to grow up. I don't think I realised, until this week, what that means."

"What does it mean?" Jake asked.

"Accepting that I know myself better than anyone else ever can. That only I can take responsibility for my choices, my actions… and my dreams."

"Sounds like a good start." She could almost hear him thinking, *but where do I fit in?*

"I realised that everything I was doing – moving to London, leaving the hotel – it was all because I thought that was what success looked like. Even Jenna's dare… she wanted me to sleep with you to get you out of my system, so I could go out on the pull with her in London." A scowl crossed Jake's face at her words, and she held back a laugh.

"But I realised, I'm not Dory. I don't want that life. And I'm not Tim, or Jenna, or even Mum or Dad or Lara. The things they want, and even the things they want for me, they might not be right. Only I can decide what's right for me." She looked up at Jake willing him to understand.

"And I thought I knew what was right for you too," he said. "I thought I needed to stay away from you. And then I changed my mind without even talking to you about it." He shook his head. "I'm sorry."

"It's okay. Because in the end, you walking away… that's what forced me to think about what I really wanted. And I figured it out, at last."

"Yeah?" Was that hope in his eyes? Molly hoped so. "So, what does a happy, successful life look like for Molly Mackenzie?"

The million dollar question.

"I started out by figuring out what I didn't want," she explained. "London… it's a great city, but it's not for me. And I need a job that's new and different every day. So… I emailed my resignation to my company. I still have to work out my notice and pack up my room at the flat but after that… there's an events job going at the Majestic hotel. Krissie, my old boss, thinks I'd be perfect for it."

"So you're moving back home?" Jake smiled. "Your mum and dad must be pleased."

"I hope they will be. I haven't told them yet," Molly admitted. "I wanted to talk it all through with you first."

"Me? Why?"

"Because the next part has to do with you." Molly took a deep breath. "The thing is, I can't keep sneaking around with you, Jake. I can't lie to the people I care about that way. Least of all you."

"I get it." Hands in his pockets, Jake took a step back. "And look, if it's too weird to have me around—"

"No, Jake. You don't get it." Swallowing hard, she moved towards him, one hand pressed against his chest. "You're one of the people I care about. And I was lying if I let you think that all I wanted was one night. Maybe that's how it started out, but it could never be just that between us, Jake. You matter too much to me."

"As an almost brother?" he asked, and she shook her head.

"As a partner. As the man who made me grow up. Who makes me feel more, think more, and want more than I ever believed possible." And now, the hardest part. "As the man I've fallen in love with."

They were the right words, it seemed. Jake swept her up in his arms, his kisses desperate, as if he couldn't get close enough to her.

"You are my family, Jake," she whispered, between kisses. "Just not the way everyone always thought."

"As long as I'm yours, I don't give a damn what anyone else thinks," Jake murmured back.

Molly smiled against his mouth. He was right. They'd found what was right for them. Now they just had to live it, together.

"I did make one more resolution," Molly said, as Jake rested his forehead against hers, smiling down at her.

"Yeah? What was that?"

"To be kissing you at midnight on New Year's Eve," Molly told him. "Next year, and every year."

"You're definitely getting better at this resolutions thing," Jake told her, and kissed her soundly.

Molly ran her hands up his back and kissed him back. In that case, she couldn't wait to see what she came up with next year.

Behind her, a cork popped out of a Prosecco bottle and she realised that the party had spilled out into the hall. It was nearly midnight, nearly a whole new year. She was kissing Jake, and she didn't care who saw.

She just knew that this new year, and every day after it, would be her best year ever.